CORE

A Romance

KASSTEN ALONSO

HAWTHORNE BOOKS & LITERARY ARTS | Portland, Oregon | MMV

Hawthorne Books
& Literary Arts

1410 NW Kearney St.
Suite 909
Portland, OR 97209
hawthornebooks.com

Form:
Pinch,
Portland, Oregon

Editorial Services:
Michelle Piranio

Printed in China
through Print Vision, Inc.

Set in DTL Albertina.

First Edition

9
8
7
6
5
4
3
2
1

Library of Congress
Cataloging-in-
Publication Data

Alonso, Kassten, 1968–
Core : a romance / Kassten
Alonso. – 1st ed.
p. cm.
ISBN 0-9716915-7-6
(alk. paper)
1. Triangles (Interpersonal
relations) – Fiction.
2. Male friendship – Fiction.
3. Mentally ill – Fiction.
4. Betrayal – Fiction.
I. Title.

PS3601.L59C67 2005
813'.6 – dc22
2004025277

For Monica, for Mavis.

In Acknowledgement

Craig Lesley: unbeknownst to you, the writing assignment you gave me planted the seed for this book; Tom Spanbauer: your compassionate guidance nurtured my vision, my spirit, and saw this book to fruition; Joanna Rose: your insightful enthusiasm for my work invigorated me time and again; to the writers in Tom's Tuesday night workshop, thank you for the fecund profundity of the criticism you offered; and Rod Grosz at Caldwell's Colonial Chapel, for your generous humorous expertise; and Diannah Anavir and Erikka Alonso-Eakin, for the blood we share; and Monica Drake-Alonso, for showing me the romance; but not least, my eternal gratitude to Stevan Allred, you sly devil you: without your unwavering faith, without your selfless death-defying act, this book would still lie fallow at the bottom of a drawer.

CORE

The corpse you planted last year in your garden,
Has it begun to sprout? Will it bloom this year?
Or has the sudden frost disturbed its bed?
Oh keep the Dog far hence, that's friend to men,
Or with nails he'll dig it up again!

T.S. ELIOT
The Wasteland: I. The Burial of the Dead

Equinox

THE MOON SPUN. THE POPLARS BORE TRINKETS OF FRACTURED
of stuttering light. The mud sucked his boot heels as he walked through
the fen. Though warm, it had rained. It would rain again.
A hundred yards down he reached the dogleg. Music sifted through
the branches overhead. He stepped his feet left right sidewise up the spongy
bank. Beyond the fen lay the ravished cornfield, harvest come and gone.
Was there really a party tonight? Was it a dream, or something else?
Ruckle and hiss of the feathered reeds. Whispers and laughter from
the damp dead corn. He looked over his shoulder the poplars their boles
sunk down into the fen. He licked his lips. He pushed his way into the
stalks toward the music the glow of the bonfire.
The cornfield surrendered to a plowed-under clearing bodies and crackle

of voices. The bonfire thrust spears at the dark shapes dancing. He stepped from the wall of cornstalks. He went along the wall toward the crowds gathered before the kegs the meat turned on spits the boiled ears of corn. The cup of beer was wet in his hand. The leaves of the stalks brushed his arm as he walked along the wall. Past the roadway cut into the field. Past the bonfire. Past more bodies danced and drunk and laughter.

The band played in a nest of cables and amplifiers and speakers on the plywood flatbed of a truck. What would happen when it rained again? Would the guitars toss sparks, spawn fledgling moons, darkness and silence? Would the bonfire hiss or scream? What would happen to him? It was here the arm slipped through the crook of his arm the key into the lock. A dream or something else, he could not look.

I cannot believe I found you here, she said. Surprised to see me?

He raised his cup the beer that stung his throat on the way down. The kind of beer that made his feet cold and wet.

No, he said.

Well if you're not surprised to see me then you must be happy to she said. Her fingers scratched his chin. I like the goatee it looks so good I almost didn't recognize you.

She held him close she took the cup of beer from his hand. She raised the cup to her lips. Bracelets slid down her wrist. His fingers brushed her thigh. She wore the cutoffs she'd had on the day she. And the warmth that was. And fragrancy of daffodils. He curled his fingers in his fist.

Where have you been? he said.

Aren't you even going to tell me how good I look without my glasses? She batted her lashes and smiled. I wear contacts now, she said. This woman I just ran into Gina she said I have the greatest eyebrows and I had to agree I mean things like that get noticed when the face isn't hidden don't you think?

The fen was the last thing he remembered, the way the moon sawed through the trees the flashing shovelblades of light the last things.

Where have you been? he said.

She took another drink. She licked foam off her lip she handed him the wet cup. Oh you know here and there, she said. Mostly up in Seattle couch surfing bumming even did a little dancing my god you would not believe how much money can be made for that sort of thing. I mean it was time I left here anyway I was going absolutely nowhere I was going insane. It's like I feel so much more at peace and freer now.

He drank down the cup of beer. Figures swayed in the dead corn. Shapes shifted to the music, drunk, they tripped around the bonfire. *And swing of a hammer, swing of a shovel. Breathless running through the fen, muddy hands clutched to his ears. Slipping on the blackened face that sweats red tears.*

You ran away, he said. There's no peace in that.

SPARKS COUGHED LOGS AND BALES OF STRAW AND BUNDLES of cornstalks tossed onto the bonfire. On the flatbed the band dinked around with sound checks before the last set. Lighters flickered Stars across the clearing. And bodies sagged to the mud. So many beers, such cold wet feet.

She leaned against him her cheek upon his shoulder. He watched the foam dwindle in his cup. Too simple to say anything. All simple took was belly and thigh and sweat of daffodil. All simple took was her foot pressed on his foot. Her breath on his throat. All simple took was. He raised the cup to his mouth.

She said, Y'know you can balance a egg on end at a pacific time during the equi, equinox. You can balance a egg so it stands up all by itself ha ha Sara n' me you know Sara right? Yeah you do. Me and Sara had her whole counter covered with all these ballast, balanced eggs. Fuck it was so amazing.

He sipped his beer. I thought that was only during the vernal equinox.

Huh?

Springtime, he said. That egg trick won't work in the fall.

Yes it does. We did it. Serious. Oh fuck man you don't know a thing, she said and pulled her arm from his arm. Beer slopped out her cup. Damn. Don't do that don't give me that look. I know what it means it means you mean you think I'm full a shit you goddamn goateed bastard fuck I really hate that fucking superior attitude you don't know shit do you.

Okay. So you can balance an egg in the fall. He blinked and laughed. What are we talking about here?

Doesn't matter anymore I got to piss. Come with me.

He laughed again.

Oh fuck you wait right here then. I just don't want you to disappear 'cause you got to dance me at least one dance before this party's through and we really need to talk so hold this for me okay? She handed him her cup.

I thought we were talking, he said.

She turned and Barefoot walked across the mud and joints of stalk and leaf and plastic cup. Her thighs ushered ghosts in the moon the firelight pale phantoms pain and paintings in his head. She dissolved into the ravaged corn. The sky began to rain.

He stood with a cup of beer in each hand. Across the clearing figures hammered poles into the mud around the truck. Crossbars were screwed into the poles. As the tarp dragged over the frame, someone screamed.

Beyond the bonfire cops in helmets rushed across the clearing Sirens and dogs Flashlights guns and shields This is the Police voices yelled the bonfire spat he ducked as rat-toothed pigs ran past swinging swastikas, all was noise and showers of light. Shadows chased and tackled. Arms raised against baton and pepper spray. You are all under arrest. He threw down the cups and backed away, into the corn.

She had not gone far. Her body crumpled between two rows. He kneeled beside her. The mud soaked cold through his knees. Mud in streaks across her thighs. The untoothed stalks barked at bodies crashed and shouted in the rain.

He ran his fingers over her scalp. Back of her neck. Not hit, only dead drunk. He took hold of her shoulders he shook her and her head bounced against the mud. Wake up, we got to get out of here. She groaned but did not open her eyes. As before. As before he saw her naked, saw her beneath him, seated on top of him, he. Was this all a dream or someone else?

Flashlights bobbed all around. He ducked down. He gripped her shoulders he dug his thumbs under her collarbones he shook her. Come on, wake up, he said. Party's over. Hey, come on, damn it.

Her eyes fluttered she raised a hand to shield her eyes against the rain. What? What?

The fucking cops, he said. He grabbed her wrists he pulled her off her back. He dug his feet into the mud he leaned backward, pulling on her arms. Come on, get up.

Where's Cameron? she said and her wrists slipped muddy from his hands he spun his arms he fell into the crackling stalks. A voice boomed on a megaphone. A siren whoop whooped. *Shovelheads sawblades swung. Mud flung in thick wet clumps. She belly pressed to he mouth a hammer swung and swung and swung and* Snap out of it, he said. He wiped the corners of his eyes. Snap out of it, or your ass is busted.

She fell back. She slapped her hands on the mud. You have to carry me, she whined. I can't walk I'm too fucked up I'm not supposed to drink alcohol y'know.

I can't carry you, he said. It's too wet. I'll fall.

Drag me.

He laughed. The third time tonight. Laughter is good for the soul is good for what ails you is good for nothing is laughter. Christ. He unbuttoned his denim work shirt he stripped it off he tied the sleeves around her wrists. He pulled hard on the shirt. Her arms jerked up from the mud.

Ow she said.

All around dogs barked Cops dragged bodies kicking through the stalks. He leaned backward he hiked his feet until the mud let go her body. He dragged her down the row. He dragged her over stones and broken stalks and stunted ears of corn. Crouched at the shadows running past.

On her back he towed her from the field, the heated voices. His feet slapped puddles like shovelblades. He shook the rain from his hair and the hair from his eyes. Near the poplars the fen His feet dished out from under him his shirt ripped Cornhusks he tumbled knees and elbows down the bank, face first into a bowl of mud. She fell on top of him laughing. He spit and coughed and Fuck. He kicked he shook her off his back. He pushed himself to his knees.

On her back, a manikin mud and leaves. Arms unfurled she thighs an open invitation. She eyes glinted scattered shovelfuls of moonlight. *Belly go weak with dying stars, breathless running through the fen. The blackened face that sweats red tears.* He spit again. His squeezed he cold mud hands into he armpits he shivered.

He said I can't drag you anymore.

She watched him. She rubbed her heels against the mud and she watched him. I really do like your beard, she said. You look just like Cameron.

HE FELT ALONG THE WALL FOR THE LAMP. HE TWISTED THE rough pebble of the switch. The bungalow was one room. On either end the kitchen the bathroom. On the dinette stacks of ceramic tile and dirty dishes. A mason jar filled with paintbrushes Wood flowers drowned in thinner. Books in stacks in milk crates around the room. Books cracked face down on the bed. The bed with blankets spilled to the floor beer bottles on the floor. Between dinette and bed the plastic sheet stapled over the hole in the wall. She pushed the door shut. The plastic sheet rustled.

My god, she said. Her muddy footprints across the dusty hardwood. I cannot believe you still have the wall torn down. How can you stand to have it all open like that?

He pulled the string hung from the ceiling. One bulb snapped yellow. Dead dark bugs in the shade. He said It's kind of nice this way, actually. It's like, I feel more at peace and freer now.

She said Yes but are you ever going to build the bedroom? Her eyes blinked in the curded mask of mud. Things chased things in her flickering gaze. She said, What I mean is.

It's nice this way, he said.

She looked down at the floor. Fernblades her hair leaves glued her chest her thighs. The way she had screamed into his mouth. The way her thighs pulled him down and further down beneath vegetable and dirt. She was manikin of daffodil. Beneath the mud she was his wife.

Well maybe we should like lay down some newspaper or something, she said. We'll get everything all muddy.

He shrugged and turned toward the kitchen. As before. What did it matter? The best-laid plans ran rootless through the fen. He pulled open the refrigerator. Breath of mold and viscid greens. He saw he did have one.

Why can't you drink alcohol? he said to the cold the buzz of light.

Oh well because of the meds I'm on didn't you know? He closed the fridge and moved toward the dinette. He cupped the egg in his palm. She said, See while I was up in Seattle the folks paid for me to see this doctor. Shrink. Whatever. Everyone always told me I was crazy you know? But to hear it from a guy who gets paid to know these things, well.

He stood the muddied egg on the table. I thought you wore your madness like a badge.

Yes but god I really was going crazy she said. I mean I had to get out of here didn't I? She held her arms to the sides. Mud dropped leaves spluttered stuck to the floor. He tried to balance the egg. The egg fell. He raised the egg again. He let go. The egg fell lazy see saw. It was voodoo. *A hammer swung and swung and swung and* Anyhow I'm on these anti-depressants, she said. Alcohol's bad news but I couldn't help myself though I mean seeing you again everything just came rushing back. Cameron.

The egg rolled and bumped across the dinette. The egg clicked against a stack of tile. He said, The egg won't stand.

That's because the time for it's already passed, she said. She watched him from behind her mask. *Time past and time present, what might have been and what has been, the wild thyme and the wild strawberry, laughter in the fen.*

So are you still doing your art work? she said.

Sure.

Well I myself just lined up the greatest job I'm going to be working on a yacht. I absolutely love sailing. Pleasure cruises fishing it's going to be so fucking cool. This guy works out of the San Juans. We've taken his ship out a few times. He wants me but he's too old he's got a kid anyways he says I'm the most natural born sailor he's ever seen. She laughed her teeth white against the brown mud. Her body. Mud and yellow leaves. Fallen apples ripe from trees, sunk down apples in the mud. She moved around the bed toward him. She laced her mucked up arm through his arm. Rage and desire Hooves pounded Mud clots kicked up rumbled in his ears.

So are we just going to stand around here doing nothing? she said. I mean, I don't know about you but I'm not that fond of mudpacks with sticks and what's this shit? pieces of cornstalk. Why don't we get cleaned up?

Their bodies wavered in the plastic sheet. He cleared his throat. You know, this is one thing I've always loved about you he said. The way you take my arm in yours. The way you hold it. The way you, you hold me. I like the way

we used to laugh. He tried to smile. Why did you have to. Go, like that?
Don't, she said.

Remember how I used to draw you in the afternoons, when the light
was best? And we'd only just gotten up from bed?

She let go his arm. Look I'm not going to make any excuses, she said.
I told you I had to get away from here.

Her eyes watched him. He could not see himself in her eyes. He was
only mud and leaves. Isn't it hopeless? he said. Wanting someone who's.
Who's long gone? He turned his face he blinked his eyes I'm sorry, I'm just,
I don't know, I'm just so tired.

She tugged on his arm. Come on. We need to get cleaned up, she said.
We need to get clean.

The bathroom where an airbrushed sun shined up in the corner. Brown-
skinned figures glimpsed through branches of swinging trees the sparks
of whiteyellowpink flowers. Daffodils and lily pads scattered patterns over
the tiled floor.

Oh my god she said I completely forgot you painted it like this.

All was green and peaceful and right. All was soft and warm with light.
As before. What did it matter? Plans could be sent screaming senseless
blackened through the fen.

He sat on the lip of the tub. He reached for the hot water tap. He twisted
the knurled ring and water sputtered the air hammer racketed the pipes
he turned the hot again and he turned the cold.

I love this tub, she said. I love to take bubble baths I love charm baths
you know where you put in rose petals and clove oil and cinnamon or
lavender or honey and you burn incense and play soft music—

I don't have any of that stuff, he said. He leaned to wedge the stopper
in the drain.

She said Well you just don't know what you're missing.

I know what I'm missing, he said. And I know when things can't be
found ever. Water gushed into the pitted enamel of the tub. Flares of rust
around the drain. When do you start this job?

Oh I should be starting it now but I decided I needed a little time to
myself to relax you know? I've had so much stuff to deal with I haven't had

I never have any time for me. Too busy. So before I hit the high seas I thought I'd come down here and see Bill and Pam and the gang. You.

The hammer swung and swung. Mud flew great clots cow flop plop plopping. Spurt and spurt of fearful breath. He filled the tub with mud he trembled breathless bloody from the fen.

You know what I really want to do? she said. Buy a motorcycle and tour the country. I've always wanted to see New England and New York I'd love that I'd have to get a big bike though a little one is a waste of time no guts no glory and nothing less than a thousand cc's.

The tub was full. He turned off the water. He glanced sidelong at her thighs. Cutoffs. There a hole. Despite cornfield and fen the mud had not reached into the hole. Her skin glowed under the muck. Glowed like a star, a ripened moon. It glowed and spun. Skin sung.

His fingers lifted from the water dripped drops Thunder from the tips Mud in the water bled Blossoms cracked open to reveal Sex in petaled silence he reached his bleeding hand that dripped mud

      to the blurred tiles

Come here he said

and ran through the fen he slipped he fell in breathless in laughter. He gripped her hips in his hands the shovel dug and dug the mist of blood the smoke of saw the Moon a ragged spinning in the hole in her cutoffs He squeezed the mud he squeezed the flesh He squeezed the hammer in his fists He pulled her goddamned closer

Just let me he said

and his fingers slid over the choked buttons of her cutoffs. He pulled the buttons open she skin White burst she pussy dark and wet Yet how else would it be and his kissed she belly and the hollows of she thighs he brushed he lips across the hair and he kissed her Ah where the moon stood Oh where the unmarred fires lay spinning

Just let me he said

No no don't she said, and I can't take that, she said, and You're going to make me, she said, and he couldn't help himself he dug his fingers in her ass he pressed he mouth where hammers and shovelblades swung sparks darkness

What happened

                   to Cameron? she said

      Please

         he whispered

              The bath is ready

and her fingers plucked and plucked his hair You got to tell me she said
She pushed herself against his face His tongue ached at the root from he
fucked her with he tongue The cracks in the ceiling in the egg yawned wider,
terror, grief, blood, birth I squeezed the shovel in my hands I dug and dug
the mud because you laced your arm through mine, you pulled me close
to whisper things that kill me with my need the way mud can fill a hole
Running through the corn Running through the fen dragging you behind
me The egg would not stand the Blackened faces sweat red tears I did what
I had to do and The Cop, the cops, would they come slipping and slopping
with their dogs their boiling eyes and razored rats teeth This is the Police
come grinding up the fen? Come here? Eventually? To claim me?

Let's get into the bath, he said against her skin.

His mud hair in her mud fingers. She squeezed his hair she pulled his
head back.

Tell me what happened to him, she sobbed.

Let's get into the bath.

Why won't you tell me where Cameron is you're his friend, she said.

He tried to reach his mouth to her pussy. She clapped her hands on his
face. She shoved him his feet kicked out the back of his head gonged Stars
against the tub his arm swung knuckles rapped the faucet. He choked and
kicked and sat up in the riled bath. The front door opened slammed the
plastic wall snapped once. Soiled bathwater burned his eyes. *Mud with
blackened faces sighed.* He sucked his breath. He sank under the water.

4

THE POLICEMAN WAS BIG. THE POLICEMAN SMELLED LIKE LEATHER. Metal hooks and buttons twinkled on his belt. The policeman wore his gun just like a cowboy. The policeman asked for Grandma.

She's makin supper he said.

Please tell her I'm here, little fellah, the policeman said.

Grandma went to the door wiping her hands on her apron. Grandma's eyes was black round the edges like she was to get a spanking. The policeman had his hat in his hands. The policeman looked down at him. Grandma looked at him too. Grandma said Go play.

But Grandma.

Git.

Out the screen door bang. Pollen floated from the trees. Pollen made things fuzzy in the pink sun. He ran past the apple trees climbed under the old gray fence ran down the slope of broomgrass and wild carrots to where the rusty cars sat. He climbed inside the old pick up truck. Bits of glass hopped on the broken seat. He reached for the bent up wheel. He twisted the wheel back and forth and cussed and kicked at the pedals. Linny was a big kid Linny reached the pedals. Linny was at summer camp. He was glad for that. He twisted the wheel and hit the dead horn.

There was a noise from the old willow trees. He climbed up on his knees to look. Somebody cried over and over. Oh. Oh. Oh. Oh. He could not see who was over there. He kicked his way back out the old pick up. He jumped to the ground. Oh. Oh. Oh.

The pink sun winked through the black cornstalks. He pretended he was an injun brave and snuck through the rusty cars. He tiptoed through the broomgrass. He peeked around a willow.

It was Roxy. Roxy's frizzy red hair was spread out on the ground. A man laid on top of Roxy. The two of them laid next to the corn. Roxy bucked her hips she tried to get up. The man had Roxy down. They jeans was bunched around they ankles. The man moved back and forth over Roxy. Roxy squealed and bucked and pulled on the man's butt. The man pulled Roxy's hair. Oh. Oh. Oh. Oh.

Grandma hollered for him to come inside. Roxy's mouth was open and her eyes shut. Roxy kicked on the ground. The man had her down. Pollen floated over the black corn. Sooner and the other dogs barked. A car started. Roxy and the man rolled side to side. The pollen floated. Sooner and the other dogs barked and the car drove up the road. Grandma hollered. Roxy cried. Roxy was looking at him.

He turned and ran.

IT WAS NOT HIS BATH DAY BUT GRANDMA MADE HIM TAKE ONE anyhow. Grandma combed his hair, even. And he had to put on his Sunday clothes. He did not see why all the fuss. Not for Ma and Pa. He did not see why everybody was so sad. Grandma pulled and tugged his tie and cussed and pulled the tie undone again. I want chocolate ice cream, he said.

They drove to the parlor. He sat on Chuck's knee. Rob and Linny and

Roxy sat in back. Grandma wore a veil. Everybody wore black. He tried to say something but Chuck just shushed him.

There was lots of people at the parlor. They all looked when Grandma and him and the others walked in. He got to sit on a sofa in front. In front was two boxes with flowers all over. And Pastor Fritz in his white robe. Pastor Fritz laid his hand on Grandma's shoulder. Pastor Fritz bent over Grandma and whispered in her ear. Grandma nodded.

Thank you Grandma said.

Pastor Fritz went up front. Pastor Fritz's voice was real loud. O eternal God in who there is no death and in whose presence we are called to live as immortal spirits, our thoughts turn to the loved ones whom we greatly miss. Their absence hath taken from us a treasure the world cannot restore. Yesterday our brother and sister were with us. Now they are with Thee.

Oh. Oh. Oh. He looked up. Under the veil Grandma's chin puckered and her neck was all red. He never saw Grandma cry before.

Pastor Fritz said, The rocks endure though the centuries pass away. The ancient hills look down upon a thousand generations. The stars shine on man in his infancy and will shine beyond his little day, beyond the strength of mind to follow.

He looked up at Roxy. Roxy's eyes was puffy red like everybody else's. Last year Roxy kissed him on his birthday. Roxy chased him through the apple trees till she caught him. He felt all tickly and he giggled. Shh Roxy said and put her hand on his knee. Roxy wore a black dress. Her legs was all freckly. Roxy and the man laid on the ground. Roxy's mouth opened and closed. Oh. Oh. Oh. Roxy hollered. The man turned his head. The man was Chuck.

The Lord bless thee and keep thee, Pastor Fritz said, The Lord make His face shine upon thee, and be gracious unto thee. The Lord lift His countenance upon thee and give thee peace. Amen.

Amen, everybody said.

People lined up for Ma and Pa. It was so funny. Why people came to see Ma and Pa sleeping in those boxes. And why everybody was so quiet and sad. Chuck picked him up under the arms. Chuck had him so he could look at Ma and Pa all laid still and white in fancy new clothes.

Pa gots stuff on his mouth like Ma wears he said. He looks funny. Why Pa gots that stuff on his face? Chuck did not say nothing Chuck just set him on the floor.

Everybody went outside. Chuck and Rob and Uncle Jack and Lloyd and Bob and other men carried the boxes to the big fat black cars. Those's called hurtses Roxy said. He watched Roxy's mouth when she talked. It was his birthday next month. He wanted Roxy to kiss him again. His thing tickled him till it hurt. He pushed his hands down in his pockets.

Everybody piled into they cars. They drove after the big black hurtses to the burying place. The big men carried the boxes to the holes in the grass. They took straps and lowed the boxes in the holes. Your ma and pa was in a accident, Grandma said the other day. They passed on. You know what that means? It means they gone to heaven to live with God and Jesus and the angels. Like Grandpa, remember? He tried to think. He only could see Roxy and Chuck in the corn.

Everybody was crowded round. Pastor Fritz in his white robe said Almighty God Our Father, we commend unto Thy everlasting mercy the souls of our brother and sister, our friends.

He looked up at Roxy. Still she was crying. He had Roxy's hand. Roxy's fingernails was painted black. The other day he watched cartoons and Roxy's door opened. Roxy walked down the hall to the bathroom. She wore a tee shirt and her undies. He could see Roxy's butt. He rubbed his thing under the blanket.

Pastor Fritz said Unto Him that loved us and washed us from our sins in His own blood, and hath made us kings and priests unto God and His Father. To Him be glory and domination forever and ever. Amen.

Amen, everybody said. A man lifted a shovel full of dirt. Pastor Fritz took a handful and shook the dirt over each hole. People cried.

Grandma and Chuck and Rob took they turns with the shovel. They tossed the dirt into each hole like Pastor Fritz. Roxy pinched some dirt with her fingers. Her dress was short and showed her legs. His thing hurt all over again. He saw Roxy's eyes frown and Roxy's mouth wide open in the pink sun. Roxy's arms hugged him and her lips kissed him. Then Roxy's hands moved down to his butt. Oh. Oh. Oh. Oh.

The dirt was cold and gritty in his hands. He turned and lifted his arms up over his head. He stared down at the boxes in the holes. He wondered how Ma and Pa would get out, and when they was coming home.

SHADOWS BODIES THRASHING WHEAT. SHADOWS BODIES weaved from sheaves, bodies rolled upon the threshing floor. Hulls and chaff and muddy heels. The drift of the flail dance. The echo of harvest drum. Dead offerings tossed to murky pond water.

He erupted from the bath. He gasped the nails and tacks and ground glass in his lungs. His hand slipped from under him He bashed his mouth on the tub he fell back in the water. He beat the tub with his elbows and floundered up again. Water slapped the tub, slopped over the sides. Water stung his nose and eyes. He Newborn brayed and sobbed for air.

Well I met this chick a couple weeks back, Cam had said. I don't know if I told you.

No.

Yeah. She's coming to the party tonight, Cam had said. Equinox, man. He coughed at the light bulb in the stained ceiling. He coughed and rolled his body out the tub. His left knee thumped on the floor he fell over on his hip. Water all around him. Red spots adrift in his eyes.

But you know man me and the band's playing tonight Cam had said Which means I ain't going to be that great a date to this chick, so.

He lay beside the tub and rubbed his mouth. His heart bubbled in his chest. Newborns wanted only darkness, wet. Newborns did not want to be dangled in the light. Didn't Cam know this of all things?

He sat up and pushed forward onto his knees. He grabbed the sink he pulled himself to his feet. He reached for a bath towel and wrapped and tucked the rough cloth around his waist. His clothing another wet heap on the scuffed linoleum. He kicked the clothing aside and hawked and spat in the sink. Red spray on yellowed enamel.

Come on man, Cam had said, It'd totally lack for her to be there by herself. Sure she knows some people but. But since you promised you'd go anyway I figured you could maybe be my stand in dig? Fetch her beers and ears a corn and shit. Tell her what a great motherfucker I am.

He stared from the mirror. He ran a hand through his hair. Plaster. Face streaked wet with plaster. He pulled down his lower lip. Blood seeped between his teeth. Blood stained his eyes. Shadows rustled in his eyes. Shadows clutched of sweat and dust. Shadows black flails beat out grains on the threshing floor. Had it all been a dream? Or something else?

I told you I didn't want to stay too long, he had said. Maybe you should find yourself another babysitter.

Cam had said Look man I know what you're thinking but believe me this chick ain't my usual. Not by a fucking long shot. Check it out she dyes her hair black not blonde. Cam had laughed. Come on man. You'd be doing me a real big flavor.

He twisted the hot water tap. Brown water turned red turned clear. Water could wash blood down the sink. But water could never get warm enough. He reached for the toothbrush the rolled up tube of paste. He squeezed a blue worm of paste onto the frayed bristles. Saw his face, asleep and dreaming under the water. Eyes open under the water. And mouth wide and drowning.

He shook his head. He leaned over the sink and brushed his teeth. Plaster stained the backs of his hands. The way Cam just smiled at him and said nothing. The way Cam smiled because Cam liked this game because Cam always won. He spat pink foam in the sink. He dipped his mouth in the stream of tepid water. He spat again and rinsed his brush and said, You're such an asshole, Cam.

So you'll be my stunt double tonight? Cam said.

He waved the toothbrush at Cam in the mirror. Just promise me this isn't some kind of set up, he said.

Cam laughed. I know you're going to have a good time man. And I bet you get a kick out a this chick. I'll drop her off later tonight.

Can't wait, he said.

HAIR DYED BLACK. JUST COVERED HER EARS. METAL BARRETTES pulled the bangs off her face. Cutoffs and green horn rims and plaid shirt knotted to show her pale belly. She had big legs and big hips, her breasts not big but big enough.

He wiped his hands on a towel. The two of them watched Cam's jeep bounce away up the old fire road. The girl waved after. He looked down at his high tops. He kicked a splinter of wood. Fucking Cam.

He said, Want a beer?

She shrugged. Why not, she said.

Got some in the fridge, in the, in the studio. In here. He stepped aside so she could enter the tin outbuilding.

She turned in place to take in the room. This is cute, she said. He moved past her on the left, toward the mini fridge beneath the wedging table. He tossed the towel on the table and kneeled and said, Well. I'm not sure how cute this is, but it does the job.

So Cameron says you do like, ceramics, she said.

Hiss when he twisted the cap off a bottle. He handed the bottle to her. Among other things, he said. He opened a second bottle and rattled the caps in his fist. Sculpture mostly. Stone, plaster. Clay. Wood every now and then. And sure, ceramic. Tiles. That's why I put the kiln in.

You sell any of this stuff? she said, and took a drink.

Just the tiles, he said. To pay the bills. He sat back against the wedging table. He sipped his beer.

She leaned against the large worktable across from him and looked around. Could use a little decor, she said.

Too distracting.

The girl shrugged. A friend of mine David has a studio downtown not so full-blown as this place yet but he does have a press for prints and woodcuts and shit.

I've always wanted a press, he said. They raised their beers to their mouths and looked around. She caught him staring and he glanced away. He shook his fist and the caps clinked.

She swayed toward the back of the studio. Bottle loose between two fingers. So this is the kiln she said over her shoulder. You say you put it in?

He rose from the wedging table and walked up behind her. Yeah, he said.

That's cool, she said. She moved past him, up the back aisle of the room. He followed. She placed a hand on one hip and looked up and down. Now this thing looks like a giant spice rack, she said. What's in all the jars?

Glazes, he said. Oxides. Whiting. That kind of stuff. She glanced over the mason jars labeled with dirty masking tape, at the smaller jars, at the bottles and bins, the sieves and mortar.

This the scale Cameron weighs his dope out on? she said, and smiled. She raised her beer to her lips. What did she look like without her glasses.

Cam told you about all that, huh?

Of course, she said. Lovers tell each other everything.

He rattled the caps in his fist. He said, I suppose.

What's this thing? she said. She pointed down at the stand that held two metal rollers. The rollers were attached to an AC motor. She reached out and spun one of the rollers.

It's a ball mill stand, he said. He pushed the bottle caps down his pocket and picked up a porcelain jug. Shook the jug and pebbles rattled inside. Ball mill, he said. For mixing glazes.

She turned and stepped over to the worktable. She said, Let's see. This is a chisel and here's a spoon and a penknife. Sandpaper. One of those dental scrapy things. Oo. What kind of a hammer is this?

He shook the pebbles in the ball mill and set the mill on the stand. It's called a bouchard, he said. Bush hammer.

She swung the hammer a couple times. It's weird it's like a meat tenderizer. These points, she said, and rubbed her fingers over the face of the hammer. What's it used for?

You use it to like. Wear away stone. It like, bruises it. Pulverizes. He drank his beer. She lay the bouchard on the table.

She said, I almost want to ask what you do for fun.

He shrugged and looked around the room. Whether it's fun or not, I can't really say. But this is what I do.

She tipped her bottle up and drank. She set the bottle down on the scale. Fumbled the balances left and right. Jesus how do you read this thing? she said and laughed. Shit. Never was any good at science or home ec or school for that matter.

So what do you do? he said.

For fun you mean? Anything and everything. Her eyebrows arched behind her horn rims. Not all at once of course, she said. Even I'm not that talented. She smiled at him. She spun and stepped around the worktable as though to measure the room. Her back to him she stared out the window. So when's this party get underway?

Oh, whenever. When it gets dark, he said. The skin looked soft on the nape of her neck. The muscles stood out at the small of her back. He said, Bonfires are more pleasing at night, huh.

Well I guess we got some time to kill, she said. Got another beer for me?

Sure, he said. He finished his bottle. He came around the worktable to where she stood. He kneeled before the wedging table and pulled open the fridge. Here you go he said and twisted off the cap and held up the beer.

Thanks, she said. She took the bottle. Her fingers touched his fingers.

He put the empties in a box beside the fridge. He rose and opened his bottle and she was close beside him. He stepped away and rattled the caps in his fist. He stared at the plaster dust ground into his knuckles. So, uh. Cam says you two've been going out for a couple weeks.

More like a couple months, she said.

How long've you been in town?

About a month, she said. She took a drink and set her bottle on the wedging table. She nodded at the window. So you live over there?

He glanced out at the bungalow. Yeah, he said. I live over there.

I'd love to live in a place like this out in the middle of nowhere nobody else around no obnoxious neighbors fuck that would be so great.

It is, he said. It's always real quiet. Nobody's voice or footsteps. Just my own.

She said, So how did you end up here?

He watched her for a moment. She stared out the window. He looked to his left out the open door, at the sunlight across the parched goldenrod outside, at the butterflies and willow trees. He took a drink of his beer and rattled the caps in his fist.

THE SKY SHOWED PINK THROUGH THE POPLARS AND WILLOWS. He led her down into the fen. Through rushes and stands of cotton grass, over dead trunks and around stiff brown stalks of fireweed, wildflowers going to seed. The ground sucked at their feet.

Yeah, this used to have a stream running through it, when I was a kid, he said. Dried up, oh. I don't know. Ten, fifteen years back. There's still patches that never dry, though.

And this is the shortcut, huh? she said behind him.

They climbed the embankment at the dogleg. Before them lay the harvested cornfield. Music fell from the sky. And the sun. From the center of the field the bonfire glowed. Bodies stumbled unseen around them, laughter in the corn.

Sounds like things've gotten underway, he said. He held his hand up front of his face he pushed through the stalks. Footfall and breath of the girl behind him. The moon a white wedge, and the stars.

They stepped into the clearing plowed at the center of the field. Bodies danced around the smoking bonfire. Bodies tossed stalks and lengths of wood and bundles of straw into the fire. Bodies lined up before fat silver kegs. The pigs roasting on spits. And dished up paper plates of meat and bread and corn. A large flatbed truck was parked at the far side of the clearing. The bed was buried under lights, banks of speakers, amps, cables. Cam shirtless in levis, cowboy boots, Cam's hand thumping against his guitar, his boot heel on the flatbed. PLUTO'S DOG, a banner said, hung across the side of the truck.

He bent and untied his high tops. Pulled his socks off with his shoes. She watched him. It can get pretty muddy, he said. She shrugged and kicked off her sandals. They placed their shoes together, away from the others. The mud was cool. The mud felt good to his feet.

Let's get a beer, he said.

They made their way to the kegs. Pushed past bodies, walked through the mud. Overhead the wedge of moon and shouts and laughter from the corn. Two big plastic cups raised above his head, he and the girl pushed their way back through the crowd, toward the flatbed.

Bodies danced before the truck. Cam bobbed his head and Cam stamped his foot and Cam smiled and sang. And the world.

The bonfire wavered the light around them. The girl drank from her cup. There was sweat on her throat. And bits of corn tassel captured by that sweat. He blinked and raised his beer.

She turned her head toward the bodies and the spears of flame. Figures darted in and out the undone corn. So this is like a yearly thing, she shouted.

Yeah, he shouted. Long as I can remember. The folks who own this field. Pagans, I think, and he laughed. He glanced from her to the flatbed, then up at the sky. It usually rains, but tonight is real clear. You can see the stars.

Oh yeah, she said. She took his arm in hers. Here turn this way. She pulled him around to the right, backs to the flatbed. She spoke into his ear. See those three really bright stars?

I'm not sure. I guess so.

Those three really big bright ones, she said and traced her finger against the sky. The triangle. See it?

He squinted. All he could think was her body pressed to his body. Yeah. I see it, he said, and pointed with her. A triangle.

The one that's farthest right is Vega, she said. It's like the brightest star in the constellation. Lyra that is. The lyre. And the one that's farthest left is Altair Altair is the eye of Aquila. That's the eagle. See the stars that form the wings and the tail?

He nodded and watched her profile. He raised his beer to his lips. Squeezed the mud between his toes. He said And what's the third star?

That's Deneb. It's one of the top ten brightest stars and the highest tip of the Northern Cross. She shook his arm and pointed. See the cross?

He looked up. He cleared his throat. Yeah, he said.

Some people call the Northern Cross Cygnus but I kind of look at them as two constellations laid over each other, she said. The lowest tip of the Cross kind of forms the eye of Cygnus or the swan in case you didn't know.

Yes, he said.

And the wings go out past the arms of the Cross. Cygnus and Aquila swim past each other in the Milky Way.

Cool, he said. Her perfume smelled like flowers.

Stars are cool, she said, and the music rose, voices shouted, hands clapped. You know what I really like about stars? He shook his head. Stars mean life after death, she said.

How do you figure? he said.

The so-called experts tell us the light we see up there is all that's left of the stars because the stars died a long time ago. But we'll be worm shit a thousand times over before the light of those stars fades out. So who's outlived who?

Guess I hadn't thought of it that way, he said. Her perfume. Daffodils.

Stars go way beyond time the way we know time she said. They blink and we're gone. Stars are immortal.

He said, Guess they're like, the closest thing we have to gods.

And nothing bothers the star, she said. While life fucks us over down here throwing in all these twists and turns and sucking us dry the star doesn't change it doesn't feel. It's got bigger things to think about it's above it all the whole rat race thing. You could be watching TV or working drive up or having sex or getting axe murdered and the stars don't even blink.

He said, Nothing astounds the stars.

Exactly, she said. What I would give to be a star. What I would give not to feel.

They drank more beer, scored a couple joints, drifted beneath the drift of the stars, drifted among the bodies, the smoke off the bonfire and smell of roasted meat, mud cool between the toes. He and the girl watched the shapes bend and kick around and around the fire.

She said, So you ever going to ask me to dance?

Cornstalks rose behind her. The flames of the bonfire flickered in her glasses. What? he said and his head spun and the music all around.

She laughed and slipped her arm through his. I said I really really love this song and I think you should dance with me. It's a party after all isn't it?

He scratched the stubble on his throat. She was close, her skin against his hand the smell of her perfume. Manikin of daffodil. I don't really dance, he said and raised his beer to his mouth. The cup was empty.

Don't be shy, she said.

I don't. I mean, I'm not. I'm not a very good dancer.

She dropped her cup to the ground. She took his cup from him and dropped his cup. We're not on TV, she said. And there are no judges. And this is a slow song. Slow songs are easy. You move real slow.

No, that's okay, really, no thanks, but she pulled him through the bodies, beckoned him away from the bonfire, toward the dead and dying corn. She faced him and pulled his arms around her. She rocked her hips side to side. Arms over his shoulders, she snapped her fingers to the music, and they turned, feet brushing, he swayed with her toward the harvested stalks, surrounded by movement and shouts and laughter. Bodies tumbled Sandbags from the corn. Bodies danced and kicked up mud. Mud on ankles, shins. Mud across bared bellies, thighs.

See this isn't so bad now is it, she said. Leaves adrift in her eyes. Stars adrift in her eyes.

No, he said and laughed. She pulled him hard against her body, her thighs, her breasts. His arms tightened around her. He tilted his face toward the sky, saw her spread those thighs in the corn. Saw shadows of the stalks on her face. Saw corn ripen among the red splinters in her eyes. And sheaves of wheat, and apples, pears. Saw her legs and arms wrapped around him, darkness cool beneath the soil. Her breath on his throat. He did not know if he should kiss this person. He did not know this person. He did not know.

Head thrown too far back, drunk and adrift, he was falling. His head snapped forward and he slipped in the mud. Shit he said and fell clutching at her, fell so his hands slid behind her thighs, fell so his face pressed into her belly. Soft. Oh, soft. The girl laughed and pushed him and stepped away. He sank forward on his hands and knees. She wagged a finger at him and turned away. Arms out, she spun in circles toward the stalks, circles away from the bright yellow firelight, circles beneath the stars.

She clapped her hands and stamped her feet. She scraped her fingers up her muddy thighs, her fingers upward over cutoffs and belly. Rubbed her palms over her breasts. Jackfruit and rose apple, hazelnut and roasted yam, soiled hands that grasped ruddy ears of corn. Her arms flashed overhead, hips swaying as to sloes ripe on the blackthorn, in sheepskin, in barley water, in communion She inseparate of the corn She a stalk was trembled rhythmic whetstones clashed on scythe blades, Body swayeing to the threshing songe, Ge's a peat t'burn the witch, surely a witch, surely a Corn maiden, an oat goddess, rye witch and wheat mother, the one not to be named, She in woman, in moon, in grain, Did she beckon or did she answer a call? Was there somewhere a grave cracked like an egg Scattered earth sole remnant of the one who lay sleeping? Awakened by stags barking to their harems of hinds, awakened by adders birthing young among spent cornfields, awakened by rude dolls weaved from sheaves, by blackberry fool and hedgerow jam Garlic and sapphires to the mud Stalks done scythed and gathered in stooks, spent stalks gathered as straw, straw to the fire, and ferns, and birch tree, and furze, she was corn dancing, she was dancing corn, he a herdsman drunken stunned at the body askew on the threshing floor, stunned by the furious flail dance, by hazel wands, by hen plants, order and valour conquered by enchantment, by enchainments of desire unresolved in time past or time present, yet surely harvested among the stars.

Take five everyone, Cam's voice crackled from the speakers. Bodies slumped to the plowed soil. Smoke drifted over the corn. The girl moved toward him, firelight in her glasses. He sat before her on his knees. He could not breathe. Here in the mud she would kneel with him.

She smiled and lay her hand on his shoulder as she walked past.

Cameron, she yelled behind. Hey baby.

He looked over his shoulder. The girl skipped once and ran through the scattered crowd toward the flatbed. Cam smiled big white teeth Cam jumped down from the truck. Cam kissed and hugged and rocked her side to side. She pressed herself into Cam's arms. Cam threw back his head in laughter, Cam's teeth white within the red dart of his goatee. The girl pointed behind her and Cam looked and saw him. Cam smiled and Cam waved.

He looked away. He rose and walked off into the dead corn.

17

FOR OVER AN HOUR HE HID AND WATCHED FROM THE TREES. When he was sure, he came out in the moonlight. He went twice round the church, like he was on just a midnight stroll. Between two rose bushes, in the shadows, in the bark dust he sat. He stopped his breath to listen. There was nobody, just him. Him who alone doeth great wonders.

Between the two roses he leaned back on his arms. He clamped his teeth and kicked the basement window with the flats of his sneakers. He raised up his knees and kicked harder. The catch broke easy. The window rattled open and fell to again. A dog barked at him in the dark. A pick up raced its engine. The moon looked like a big old onion and he wiped his mouth of sweat.

He sat still a minute but there was nothing else. He rolled over on his stomach. Bark dust poked him through his tee shirt. He pushed himself backward so his legs fell into the basement. He slid his chest and shoulders and head through the window and his sneakers clapped on the floor. His gut burned some from the sill. He opened the window again and bark dust spilled like dead dried bugs as he reached for the can of gasoline.

He said, Everyone shall be salted with fire.

The moon shined down through the basement window. The can he set at his feet. He pulled the penlight from his back pocket. He gave the lens a twist. The light blinked a couple times before it showed the empty fruit crates and cartons of clothes. There were stacks of prayer books and hymnals, stacked chairs and parlor furnishings, even four or five pews.

He wiped his wrist across his forehead. His tee-shirt stuck to his back. His throat was all dry and hoarse like he'd been yelling a long time. He shined the light down on the gas can. Burs were fastened to his tee shirt and his jeans and there were splinters of bark dust, too. Everything would burn to the ground.

How when him and Linn were just kids and Linn had all kinds of tricks with fire. How Linn would be all smiles as he closed his mouth round a lit match. All the kids going oh and aw when he opened his mouth, the match smoky and Linn laughing with his breath full of sulfur. How one time he stole a box of matches and hid down in the junked cars and tried Linny's trick and hollered and ran with his hands clapped to his mouth.

How Linn could smoke from the lit end of a cigarette, Linn smiling and smoking and the butt stuck out and twitching some between his teeth. All Linn's pals thinking he was so special. Sure, Linny had lots of tricks. But they were just tricks, kid stuff, not even real magic. Unto him lay the power to scorch men with fire.

He bent to fetch the can of gas. The penlight he stuck in his mouth. The can he shook in both hands and the gasoline sloshed around. It was like the gas was laughing inside the can, tickled by getting shook up, waiting its turn. He unscrewed the cap and dropped it on the floor. He moved toward a stack of cartons. With one hand on the handle and the other on the bottom he tipped the can forward. The can gulped like it was drinking, only the can wasn't drinking. It splashed gas out on the cartons and furniture and books. Gas splashed the garden tools hung on the walls and splashed across the floor. He took care not to get any on him.

He went from one corner of the basement to the next. Sweat made his scalp itch. The penlight was making his jaw ache the way he bit it between his teeth. The smell of gas got him all dizzy and he couldn't stop himself thinking of Cam's eyes. The way Cam's eyes were so pale they looked white. It was like Cam had eyes that gave him secret powers. Cam could see in the dark and could see through walls and girls' skirts and panties and into tomorrow. He tried to blank his mind out sometimes, when Cam looked at him. When Cam ran a hand through that blond lick of hair and looked at him with those milky blue spooky eyes. When Cam looked at him like he was trying to see inside his head.

The thoughts of the wicked are an abomination to the Lord, he said.

He stood under the broke open window. The empty can he set on the floor. He dug in his pocket for the matchbox all crushed and damp with his sweat. He hoped it wasn't too wet. He pushed the end of the box and out the little drawer slid. He pinched a matchstick and squeezed the box closed between his thumb and finger and the moon just sat up there with its eye on him.

Things didn't have to be like this. He'd tried other ways. Down the slope he'd crawl to the junked cars. Off with his shirt and jeans and shorts and he'd lie on the front seat and roll back and forth on the blue bits of busted windshield. It helped, but not enough. Neither did it help to cut his stomach with a razor blade. He'd ask forgiveness and please don't cast me to hell it ain't my fault innumerable evils have compassed me about and he'd make the cuts on his skin. But when Grandma started asking why the bloodstains on his laundry and then at the beaver pond he took off his tee shirt and Cam pointed and swore, and even Roxy crouched above him in her red print dress, he knew he had to find another way. A secret way, a way that would make everybody pay. Because everybody was a hypocrite and an evil doer and every mouth spoketh folly. But mostly God.

He scratched the matchstick on the striker. There was a snap and the flame. The gas was all wet and glittery in the beam of the penlight. For wickedness burneth as the fire. It shall devour the briars and the thorns, and shall kindle in the thickets of the forests. It is a fretting leprosy. Thou shall burn it with fire.

When it had burnt itself halfway, he dropped the match to the floor.

SO, WHY'D YOU DO IT? HE SAID. WHY'D YOU GO AND DISAPPEAR like that?

He sat on the sandy ledge of the beaver pond, in a spot where the sedges and the cattails had got torn out. His feet hanged over the water. The sun was hot and caught his eyes with fire.

Cam said, I didn't disappear.

Cam stood with his back to him. Cam stood at the diving end of the diving plank. I told you I was off camping with my old man. Spur of the moment type shit didn't have time to alert the mayor whoop dee do. Cam rode up and down on his toes so the plank bounced Cam a little. Ain't like I was hoping to get my face on a milk carton or nothing, Cam said.

Yeah, but you didn't tell nobody where you got off to, he said. We was all worried about you. And your mom. Gosh Cam. Your mom was in a real bad way.

Cam began to jump up and down on the plank. Cam pumped his elbows to the sides and the plank yawned under him and Cam sprang in the air with his arms up like he was going to fly away. Cam tucked his knees and somersaulted and kicked out the tuck and cut the water with his smooth brown arms. There was a slap and a spit flew, then only ripples. Cam did not come up.

He took a deep breath and held it. Water dripped some, back of his neck. Across the pond the leaves of the ash trees shook and flickers called from the branches. Cam did not come up.

The bluff curved like an egg out from behind him. The rocks made broken steps to the sky. On the left the face carried on past the ashes. On the right it petered off well shy. From the end of the diving plank you could see the cornfield wide of the ashes and the bluff. There wasn't much to look at now, but in ten or twelve weeks the corn would shine bright as the water. The tassels all shook with fire. When hotter days came he would hide in the corn. He'd lie on his back and listen to the things that ran up and down the rows. He would hold his breath when Roxy called his name. He'd lie absolutely still lest he burst into flame.

The sun bore down on him like an ant been left in a mason jar. The breath sat on his heart. He clenched the sand in his fists. Cam did not come up.

He couldn't hold it anymore and he coughed out his breath. He counted all the way to twelve Mississippi before Cam broke for air. Cam gasped and shook his head and laughed. The bluff faces laughed with Cam. The faces hawked strong smooth strokes as Cam swam to him.

When he reached the shallows, Cam stood. The water streamed down his body. Cam stared with those milky blue spooky eyes. Christ you'd a let me drowned wouldn't you? Cam said.

He looked to the place where the creek seeped out the pond and cut through the ash trees. He said, You had to know everybody'd be worried about you.

Cam grabbed the sand and hoisted himself onto the ledge. Cam shook his head and water sprayed all over. Say man toss me that towel Cam said.

He picked up the green towel and handed it to Cam. Cam rubbed the towel over his blond hair and over his shoulders, his arms and stomach. Cam's chest rose and fell all brown in the sun. Cam said, Okay look man I admit I didn't think things out on this one. Same time there wasn't no harm done. The way people bugged just shows we could all use a good mindfuck every now and again. Keep us loose. My mom of all people could sure use one. It's like a karma thing and I can just see Mom wringing her hands and wringing her bottle and saying Where's that boy a mine he's all I got because I'm all alone here since I dumped his old man and booty hooty hoo. Cam laughed. Kind of funny, karma, ain't it? Cam said. The way things are always going around and coming around?

He stared at the scars on his stomach. They'd all healed over but a couple were still red. How last night when the fire had run along upon the ground. How it had run round the basement and had run back at him like Indians on the warpath, eating things down to the shadows. How his sneakers pedaled the wall and his fingers raked up the bark dust and he could feel the heat all wet on his back and he wondered if the furnace would blow and if he'd be able to get out in time.

He looked up at Cam. He said Thought you maybe disappeared on account a what happened with the baseball team.

Cam's eyes shined like lamps of fire. He felt Cam's eyes try to light the insides of his head. He looked away. Cam laughed. No man, Cam said, I don't give a shit about the baseball team. I took off because I never get to see my old man no more. And he's growing up so fast. Cam laughed and punched him on the arm.

But Cam, he said. Everybody knows you lost your scholarship.

Wedged into the sand behind Cam was the water bottle that didn't have water but did have vodka and soda pop. Cam stretched out and fetched the bottle and sat up and popped the cap with his thumb. Shit happens, fecal matters, Cam said. Cam raised the bottle and drank.

But that was the only way we was getting into the same school. Like we been planning?

Cam belched and licked his lips. Aw fuck school, Cam said. Fuck school and fuck baseball man. Hell I'll just play a guitar.

But you could of gone so far, he said. Mr. Randolf says you could of won the Cy Young someday. You could of been a real star.

Cam said, A star? and blinked his milk blue eyes. Don't you get it? I am hindoo baby. Bad luck and fucked days, they just roll right off me. Check it out. So what if I got kicked off the baseball team. So what if I lost the big bad scholarship. I don't give a shit about college. I don't give a shit about the majors. For chrissakes baseball's a game for kids ain't it? Cam took a drink and smacked his lips. Cam tipped the bottle like he was making a toast. All getting kicked off the baseball team means is it's time to do something else. Like learn how to play guitar. Start a band. Make a bazillion and be found dead with a couple hookers and so much coke it'll look like we got rolled in flour. Cam took a drink from the bottle and belched again. Here man.

No, he said, and he waved away the bottle.

Just have a sip man. One little sip. It's hot out.

He pushed Cam's arm away. I don't want none, he said. Butter and honey shall I eat, that I may know to refuse the evil, and choose the good.

Cam's eyes stared like chips of ice in his head. Onward Christian soldier,

Cam said. Goddamn. You ought to be a priest or something. You got the guilt for it. The scars too.

He felt his face burn. He smelled the smoke and the gasoline in his hair and saw steam come up out his skin. Cam grabbed his shoulder so he could push himself up. Cam's body looked like it was carved out of caramel. Next to Cam he was soft and pale and dead.

Cam said, Check it out man. The possibilities in this life are endless is all what I'm trying to tell you. Baseball ain't the start or the end of the world or nothing. Not when the world's a big old oyster I'm going to suck up one pearl at a time. Live in the now you know ain't that what they say? Live in the now. Be free. Fuck man. You ain't even taking care a your own now.

He looked up at Cam. Pollen drifted round Cam's head. Cam smiled down at him and drank from the bottle. What do you mean? he said.

Cam said, You know what I mean. Today's the most important day of our young lives and you're going to spend it – what? Canning peaches with your grandma?

I already told you I couldn't find no date.

You had Jenny twisting on the hook. She'd a pooped if you gave her the work order.

I couldn't take her, he said, That girl's a tramp. She's done it with everybody. Even you.

Cam's laugh bounced all round the broke up shell of the bluff. The ashes rustled their leaves. The flickers went wic wic wic hidden in the green. The creek trickled into and out the beaver pond and the sun beat on his head. Everything laughed at him.

He pulled his feet out the water and swung his legs up onto the ledge. Reckon I didn't want to go to no prom anyhow, he said. It ain't nothing except evilness, drink and adultery. He stood and went through the reeds and hoppers scattered and a snake rasped off into deeper cover.

Hey man, Cam said.

He walked out on the diving plank. The plank bobbed some with each step. He curled his toes over the end. Mats of water fern and glossy clouds of duckweed floated on the water. Round the pond purple loosestrife grew even thicker than last year. And no fingerlings hatched this season at all.

The beaver pond was dying. His folks were dead. Everything shall be salted with fire.

Cam clapped his hands and said, Hey man come on this is dumb you got to go. Missing your prom's bad mojo ain't you heard the news? It's like a unfinished chapter type thing. You'll be unfinished and the rest of your life'll be in limbo. Come on man you want to go. You can wear your old man's tux and take your Aunt Roxy. She ain't too bad. She's what twenty-five, thirty? Come on man. Say you'll go.

He raised his arms out to the sides. He took a breath and jumped up and down till the plank dipped heavy under him. Drops of water flipped off his skin. His head already hurt from the sun and hurt worse when Cam called his name. His knees came apart and he caught the plank wrong and the plank hucked him. He fell up in the air. His back arched so his feet went over his head. His calves slapped the water and the water made a plunging sound in his ears. It was cold, and for a second he thought he might burst to steam and float away. Instead pondweeds brushed on his skin and he opened his eyes. Bubbles floated up all round him. How last night he skinned out between the two roses and the sweat and smoke made him blind as he ran for the trees. How the windows busted and the flames were like hands that clawed their way up out the basement of the church. How he looked down and saw the cuffs of his jeans were on fire and he thought to let it be till his skin was all black on him, his bones burnt up with heat.

He let out his air. Bubbles spilled up from his mouth, he sank. He wondered if Cam was holding his breath. He looked up and saw the sun and even the trees. Everything was so bright up there, and where he floated it was dark.

28

SKIP AND STUTTER OF STONES. FOOTFALLS ON THE FIRE ROAD.
He poured plaster into the coddle. A silhouette rose at the open door. The
silhouette spoke his name. In the shadowed palm the badge the gold leaf
borders that glinted the hollow sunlight. That whirled, the blade of a saw.
He sank the mixing bucket into the rinse barrel. His hands shook, clotted
and slick with plaster.

    Sorry?

    I say, you got yourself quite the operation here Son, the cop said. Quite
the little hideout.

    His hands hung wet at his sides. His sweatshirt on the floor. He said,
Of sorts. Yeah.

    Had to leave my vehicle at the bottom a the road, the cop said. If I'd a known you was this far back I'd a signed out a jeep or a 4×4. That walk's about a mile ain't it?

Something like that he said.

The cop said, And all them potholes. Almost looks like they been dug on purpose. The cop laughed. Hoo. Awful warm day out here. Mind if I come in and talk a minute?

He tucked his hands under his arms. Plaster smeared across his bare ribs. No, Sir, he said.

The cop chuckled and stepped up into the studio. The cop wiped his neck with a kerchief. The cop smiled at the naked armatures and tore open bags of plaster. At the abandoned busts and broken molds. The cop peeked at the fresh plaster filled the coddle. Peered toward the back room where the kiln sat. Smiled at the shelves full of glazes.

Quite the operation, the cop said and dabbed the kerchief on his forehead. The cop's face was pockmarked, red and damp from heat. The cop smiled with teeth large dried corn kernels. Hoo my. I tell you I could sure go for a smoke right about now. Would you mind?

He leaned against the worktable. No, he said.

You're a real lifesaver Son, the cop said and pawed in his sport coat. Withdrew a hard pack. Shook up a smoke. The cop pinched the butt between withered lips. Held out the pack.

No, thank you, he said.

The cop said, Smart kid. I know I should give these buggers up but. Hell. Retirement's only five years off so why stop now? Laughter. Hairy hand replaced the pack pulled out a silver lighter. The dark tail of the pistol curled from the cop's armpit hidden and exposed and hidden a stripper and the tease. I tell you you been a hard one to find, the cop said. Metal snap of the lighter. Butane spark and crackle of flame. White tendrils snaked toward the open window. Aw well, the cop said. Least your name's the last one on my list a interviews.

His mouth had gone dry. He licked his tongue to free his lip from his teeth. He said, What can I do for you, Sir?

The cop blew smoke toward the ceiling. Reptile blink of watery eyes. Sweat spotted the cop's shirt on either side of his tie. Lord if this ain't a fine way to pass the day, the cop said. Bet it's real peaceful out here. His sweatshirt lay on the floor. A crow cawed from the fen.

Got a workshop a my own, the smoking mouth chuckled. I make chairs tables. Dressers. Nothing fancy or arty but they work. Functional I guess. Leastways it's better than seeing a headshrinker. The yellow teeth smiled broad but he wasn't buying any of it. Smoke pricked his eyes. The cop pointed the cigarette toward the window. That your place yonder?

He unfolded his arms and rose from the worktable. The plaster on his hands was drying, becoming warmer, brittle confection, divinity.

The property belongs to my family, he said. I'm a tenant, more or less.

Anybody else home?

There is no one else. I live alone.

The cop laid his palms on the wedging table and nodded at the window. Looks like you're adding a room, the cop said.

Yeah, he said.

The shovel swung and swung. Sawblade spun and sung. He bent for the sweatshirt scabbed with polychrome and plaster. He pulled the shirt over his head. He breathed the cop's smoke and spiced cologne. He cleared his throat. So, uh. What can I help you with, Sir?

Hairy hand reached into sport coat unveiled pen and pad. I'd like to talk to you about Cameron Davis, the cop said. I understand he was a friend of yours.

The right to remain silent. Silent. Anything you say can and will be the right to remain silent. You have the right to an attorney and that will be used against you. If you cannot afford an attorney one will be Can and will be Will be used against you. Remain silent. Anything you say. Remain silent. Silent. The crow cawed from the green trees.

He said, Is Cam still. Has he been found?

Lips puckered Cigarette crackled red. The kernels of teeth flashed breathed smoke watched him with rummy blinking reptile eyes. Afraid not Son, the cop said. Did the cop already know, was this all just for show, his back-up crouched in the underbrush, the fen, in the trees and on the bluff, rifles with scopes and shotguns tear gas Awaiting the signal No one gives a fuck if they take you alive as long as they take you. Remain silent.

He said, Well, I, I'd like to. I'd like to help anyway I can, Sir.

The cop nodded and flipped open the notepad. Pushed the pages up with his thumb. Okay let's see here, the cop said. Cameron was last seen. Two months ago. It was on the seventh and that was a Tues, no a Wednesday. The cop tapped the pen on the pad. Now Son. Have you seen or heard from Cameron at all since then?

I. No. I don't, I don't think I have.

The cop said Can you recall the last time you did see him?

He coughed into his fist. The plaster cracked along the back of his hand. I'm not sure, he said, It's been so long. Maybe not since. I don't know, like. Maybe last fall? He shrugged and scratched his neck. I'm just not sure.

The cop nodded. I understand, he said. But just think a minute now.

I'm trying, but. It's all so. It's so strange. I can't think what could've happened to him.

The cop held up his cigarette. The cop smiled. Got something I can put this out in Son?

He shook his head. You can, uh. You can put it out on the floor.

The cop dropped the ailing smoke to the cement floor. Shoe ground back and forth, a bug. The cop dug in his sport coat. Bit down on another cigarette. Snapped open the lighter. Smoke huffed from the cracked lips the lumpy nose Face of craters Face like the moon This is the Police.

What?

The lighter snapped closed. I say, maybe you remember Cameron ever mentioned leaving town, the cop said.

No he said, Only in terms of his band. Going places and stuff.

The cop flipped through the pad. Yes right right. Cameron was a musician. Were you in the band too?

No.

Hairy hand scratched the pen on the notepad. Flipped through the pages. So Cameron never talked to you about leaving town, the cop said. Do you know of any trouble he might a been in?

He rubbed a rough hand across his chapped lips. Chunky white gloves of divinity concealed his hands protected him from evil pure and sweet Dear god give me the strength to Remain silent.

No, he said. He cleared his throat.

The cop said, Son're you feeling okay? You're looking kind a pale. Maybe the cottage'd be more comfortable.

I'm fine, I. Just a summer. A cold, I think. Weather got so warm all of a sudden and everything and. And.

Can I make a suggestion? the cop said. Take a deep breath and relax. I'm only here to uncover the whereabouts of a friend. His family and other friends're all worried and would want to know right? They all wanted to help in any way they could.

I want to help.

That's good Son. But just relax a little. Think back. Any information you have might be just what's needed to develop a solid lead. I can't empathize that any stronger.

I understand, Sir, he said. I'm, it's just. He ran a frosted hand through his hair. He said, Cam and I used to be a lot closer, you know, and. And. We saw each other more. In high school we were pretty close. Best friends, I guess. But we grew apart. Older. You know how it happens. See a person less and less, until you're not sure when you. When the last time was you saw them. He shrugged and scratched his throat. I don't know. This is all so strange, he said.

The cop puffed his cigarette. Beads of sweat on the cop's forehead. Sweat stained the collar. I hear what you're saying Son. I know you're trying your best. Maybe what we need is some kind a record. A checkbook or maybe a date book. A journal. Something a that nature.

I don't have any of those things, he said.

Are you sure you ain't got something to jog your memory?

Metal shriek and spume of sparks. Walk deeper, foot soundless, into the fen.

I don't keep records, he said. I don't save things.

How about your job?

Well. I make tiles. Small, private contracts. But I haven't had any work since. Well. For a while now.

So you got no way to account for your time, the cop said. No records invoices receipts. Utility bills?

Uh. I have a generator and a well, so. No.

Maybe a friend or a relative a yours might remember. Someone who sees you regular. Someone you might a been with last time you saw Cameron.

He picked at the white frosting caked his fingernails. I mostly keep to myself, and. Well. I haven't seen my family for. He rubbed the back of a hand across his mouth. He laughed. God, I can't even remember the last time, he said. I just. I don't see people.

The cop nodded and smiled but his neck was red. The cop scratched pen on pad. Red welts razor burn on the cop's throat. And mumbled knot of tie.   The cop thrown on his belly down on the floor. Huffing and twisting side-to-side, thick wrists bound behind his back. Cigarette hanged off the cop's lip. The scarred sack of face stretched obscene the cop hollered You ain't going to get away with this.   But how to take the cop by surprise.

Cameron had a girl didn't he?

The crow rattled outside. He shook his head. What?

I say Cameron had a girlfriend.

Cam had a lot of girlfriends.

Well this one's been dogging me about the investigation. Hoo. Awful single-minded that girl. Leastways she was up till a few weeks back. Now looks like she's up and disappeared too, the smoking mouth the kernelled teeth the reptile eyes said. The cop dropped the half-spent cigarette to the floor. Ground it out. The cop lit a fresh cigarette. Withered lips puffed Smoke and spiced cologne Hey it's Everyone's favorite uncle Don't be fooled This is the Police.

Now you suppose she might a gone off to meet up with Cameron? the cop said.

How would I know that? he said. I told you, Cam and I. We're not close anymore. I don't even know which girl you're talking about. For all I know, they could both be. They could be anywhere.

He swallowed, scratched his neck.   She naked sprawled down in the fen. Her thighs yawned luminous under the gray sky.   The way he rolled with her in the mud. The way she clutched him to her and screamed in his mouth. Had she been the one to give the cop your name?

And what else did she say? Don't think about it. Don't see it in your eyes. Don't. The smile on Cam's lips. The damp on Cam's lips. Cam upon the floor. Christ, think of something else. Marble angels meditate on the Instruments of the Passion. Cupid carves his bow from Hercules' war club. You are free to be silent, be cloaked with divinity.

Son, the cop said. Smoke curled around the cop's face. The tip of the cigarette rasped red. Son, the cop said, voice low and flat a dog crouching through underbrush, Son, the cop said, Do me a favor and put the hammer down.

What?

I said put down the hammer. Now.

He stared at the stud-toothed mallet in his fist. The crow hooted outside. It's called a bouchard, he said.

Put it down Son, the cop said.

He lay the bouchard on the worktable. Sorry, I. I wasn't going to. I'm just nervous, is all.

Maybe we should talk in the house. Might be more comfortable for you.

No.

Well why don't we talk outside then the cop said. Get some fresh air.

He gazed at the plaster on his hands. He said, Okay.

The cop raised an arm toward the open door and smiled. After you Son.

He hunched his shoulders and stepped out into the pink sunlight. There a gallows, a jeering crowd. Bullet in the back. The shovel dug and dug. The way his clothes coughed flames black smoke ashes darkness. The way he shivered alone in the tub. Wild thyme unseen and wild strawberry, laughter from the fen.

Must get kind a lonely, the cop said. Living out here all by yourself.

He shook his head. I like to be alone, he said.

Maybe so. But no one likes to be lonely, the cop said. Shimmer of rummy eyes in the pink light. You don't like to be lonely do you Son?

No. Of course not. Loneliness isn't a desirable way for anyone to. He folded his arms. But, like all emotions, loneliness comes and goes. It has nothing to do with being alone.

The cop nodded. Tapped pen on pad. You seem like a nice kid, the cop said. Guess it's hard to understand why someone like you'd want to keep shy a others.

There's nothing to understand, he said. I'm not interested in relationships. I don't have the time to. To put into meeting people. To going through the steps it takes to fall in love.

Smoke wafted around the nodding head. What about the folks you already love? What about your family?

He shrugged. My work takes my mind off so many things.

That's a real shame, the cop said. Stray too far from your loved ones and you forget where you come from. Forget who you are.

I keep telling you, I don't need anybody, he said. I know enough about myself to know that much.

But Son. Everyone needs love.

He laughed. He laughed at the rummy teeth and kernelled eyes, the big hairy hands and the spiced cologne of good ole Uncle Copper. He laughed at the smiling yellow malevolence. The crow that chattered in the fen.

You don't know what I need, he said. He laughed again.

The withered lips frowned. The cop shrugged dropped the butt to the gravel. Ground it dead.

Well I was hoping to get a bit more help from you, the cop said. Here's my card. It's got my office phone and pager. If you think a anything and I mean anything don't be shy to call. Okay?

He stared down at the card. Flipped the card over and back. He said, I don't have a phone.

Pocked cheesecloth face stretched grimace good humor. Shoo. You ain't going to make life easy on a old son of a gun like me are you? the cop said. Aw well. Reckon if I need to get in touch again I'll know where to find you.

He scratched his neck. Yeah, I. I don't get out much.

The cop laughed and mopped the kerchief on his neck. Yeah I best sign out a jeep next time. Kind of a long walk. Old legs like mine I tell you. The cop held out his hand. We'll be seeing you Son. Take care a yourself.

Yeah, he said. He reached with his own hand fragile in a glove of cracked divinity. The cop's grip big and warm. I'm sorry I wasn't much help, Sir.

Well like I said I am too but. Just sleep on it. Think about it. Something always comes to light. The cop clapped him on the shoulder The Patient Reassuring Uncle and turned toward the fire road. The cop turned back. Oh and one more thing.

Yeah?

Go see your folks, the cop said. If you can't remember the last time, it's been too long.

He looked beyond the cop to the green cloister of the trees. He said, We'll see.

The cop turned away. Clumsy apish footfalls crunched and kicked gravel and got smaller and died. And would those hairy hands bend for a sample of the fire road, put it in a plastic baggie Exhibit A to be compared with the mud found on Cam's jeep? And would those yellow kernel teeth leer into every corner of your life until one day that terrible leer comes back again to speak your name? Would the plaster that caked your trembling fists be enough protection when the time came?

The crow laughed. He dropped the cop's card. He picked a stone from the ground and flung the stone into the poplars. Rustle of leaves. Again the laughter. He stumbled toward the fen. He fell to his knees and retched and black spots peppered his eyes.

5

HIM AND LINNY RAN FOR THE WOODS. HE HAD THREE PENNIES
Linny had five. Grandma gave them even Steven but Linny stole one of
his. Finder's keepers Linny said.

Him and Linny ran for the woods. They ran down the path with hard
ruts from bikes when the path got muddy from the rain. Grasshoppers
snapped brown and green across the path. A long ways off the train whistled.

He ran behind Linny. Linny was a big kid Linny ran fast. Grandma said
for us to buy candy, he said.

Linny stopped and Linny laughed. Linny's face all freckly. Grandma
said for us to buy candy, Linny smarted back. Linny poked him with his
finger. What are you a wiener?

Shut up, he said. He slapped at Linny's hand.

Linny poked him in the shoulder again. You're a wiener Linny said. A little wiener boy.

His face got hot. No I ain't. You shut up.

Wienerwienerwiener, and Linny stepped on his foot Linny pushed him he fell down. Last one there's a rotten turd, Linny said. Linny ran into the woods.

That ain't fair, he hollered. He chased after Linny through the trees. He tripped and fell over tore open bags of trash and a blowed out tire. He climbed over a big gray log. He pushed through the bushes to the railroad.

Linny was on his knees in the broomgrass by the tracks. The train wiggled in the sun. The chimney puffed black smoke. He dropped down close by Linny. The ties smelled hot and oily. He opened his fist. The pennies stuck to his skin. There was dirt in the lines of his hand. He picked the pennies from his hand and laid them one two three on the rail.

Linny said, Spread them out Stupid. You got to give them room to smoosh.

I know it he said. He used his finger to push the pennies apart. Closer came the whistle and the shushing of the train. He got up and ran back to the woods. The pennies shined. He stood in front of a big bush so the leaves scratched him on the neck.

Linny waved his arms and hollered. The train hooted and hammered down the tracks. The ground shook the sky got black. The air was heat and smoke and grease. The wheels of the train was big and spun and the broomgrass pushed all flat. He put his hands on his ears and hollered but he couldn't hear. The train was noise and speed and scare. The train was everywhere the train was gone.

He chased Linny for the tracks. The pennies was squished and long and flat. Hoo, you can't hardly see Abe's face no more, Linny said. Linny swiped all the pennies off the rail into his hand.

Hey, those's mine!

Linny shook the pennies in his hands. The metal clinkle clinked. Finder's keepers Linny said.

His eyes burned. I'm tellin Grandma.

Linny laughed and shook the pennies crickets by his ear. You do and I break your face, Linny said.

Gimme back my pennies, he said.

Look, he's cryin, Linny said. He's a big baby. A big fat crybaby. Linny shook the pennies in his hands.

Gimme them back he shouted. He ran at Linny. Linny just laughed and pushed him. He waved his arms and fell on the ground rocks and sticks in his back. He rolled over tears in his eyes. He grabbed a round green stone. Linny threw the pennies to the ground. Linny picked up a hunk of concrete.

Go ahead just try it Linny said. Linny smiled so his eyes got slits his teeth hardly showed.

Gimme back my pennies, he said. He cried he waved the stone at Linny. Make me you baby, Linny said. The sun shined on Linny's head Linny's hair was red. Linny tossed the concrete up and down in his hand. Linny sang, Cry baby, cry baby, cryin all the time.

Shut up!

Wiener baby wiener baby, Linny sang. And Linny laughed.

He yelled and threw the green stone. The stone bounced on the ground and skipped the tracks. Linny hopped sidewise Linny hucked the concrete.

Stars busted in his eyes. He wobbled all dizzy like when Chuck airplane spinned him he had no legs he fell on the ground. He fell on the ground. The ground. Nighttime and stars. A voice hollered Ma. Pa.

He opened his eyes. Linny was black in the sun. Linny poked him with his foot. Linny said, Aw, you're okay. You're a tough little shit, ain't you?

His arms and legs was awful heavy. His face was all wet too. Flies buzzed round his head. There was red on the rocks by his head. Red on his fingers when he touched the split open mouth tingly stars in his forehead. He sat up he fell over. I'm tellin he said.

You just cut your head's all, Linny said. Ain't that bad.

He tried to sit up he fell over. I'm tellin Grandma, he said with his ear to the ground.

Linny said Shit and Linny flung his arm at him. Pennies clinked and skipped over his legs. Fine, Linny said, You got your share you baby. But you ain't tellin Grandma I got you bloody because I'll just say you was throwin rocks first.

He kicked his feet to sit up. He blinked at the red in his eyes. He blinked at the sky.

Linny looked back over his shoulder Linny went into the woods. Don't tell Grandma you hear? Linny's voice from the leaves.

He pushed the ground with his hands. He stood up. Red spots on the rocks. Red spots on his tee shirt and his legs. He poked at the split sore mouth. He picked up the smooshed pennies and put them in his pockets. He was going to buy candy like Grandma said.

A plane went slow across the sky. The plane looked white and cold in the blue. It didn't make any noise. The plane made him safe and sleepy. Ma. Pa. Grandma said Ma and Pa went to heaven.

His face all wet he blinked at the plane. He waved and hollered Hi Ma. Hi Pa. He hoped Ma and Pa was in a window where they could see him.

27

SHADOWS RUN FROM HUZZAH AND SICKLE. SHADOWS COWER in the barn. Reapers tie sheaves in the shapes of rude maidens. Dogs crouch barking at the last stand of corn. Awry. Amiss. Awake.

He sat up in the tub gasping. Water and snot sputtered from his mouth. Briars thrust up under his ribs He coughed and coughed his Newborn throat tight as a pin. Muddy bathwater slapped the worn enamel. Spilled applause upon the floor. He fell back against the tub. He bared his teeth his breath sawed at the yellow bulb the cracked ceiling Jesus Christ.

With his toe he wedged the stopper from the drain. The drain gulped once. He rubbed stars in his eyes. He ran his hands through his hair. Someone had been in the tub with him. A body had curled its soft belly around him. Pondweeds Whispers brushed his ear. The girl. She had danced in the spent cornfield, had drawn him from the safety of the bonfire. She had pulled him deeper into the bath with her softness, her whispers, daffodil.

The breath whistled in and out him. He rolled himself over the lip of the tub. Water scattered Coins across the floor. On his knees and hands on the unraveled mat his fingers and wrists slick with mud. The shadows bound in sheaves. Shadows Raincharms cast to the spring. And who would cut the navel string?

He grabbed the tub and pushed himself to his feet. He turned toward the mirror. The face in there. The face watched him. Bloodless and bloated. Purple shadows ringed the eyes. Plaster in the hair drenched always. He bent over the sink he turned the hot water tap. Water spit brown from the spigot. The water cleared. He rubbed his palms under the stream.

Cam said, You got to be there tonight man. Fuck all the lame ass excuses about your work. Take the night off. Drink a few. Fucking enjoy yourself for once in your life would you?

Tendrils of mud spun down the drain. Water down the dark open mouth. How he had almost drowned again. Beneath ripple and rise, among whispers and softness, drowning.

I'll be there, he said.

POLISHED BRASS AND STAINED WOOD, RAFTERS STUFFED with leaves. Ceiling hung with crepe paper pumpkins, black cats, and witch hats. Owls and bats. The floor sodden and scuffed from years of boot heels. He shook the rain from his hair. A hand unfolded before him. He fumbled in his pocket. He lay some bills in the open palm. The hand disappeared. Back into the dark dim swirl down the drain.

Onstage Cam wrung his guitar and shouted obscene cantations. Cam in frilly laced shirt and black trousers, red kerchief tied around his head. Cam bobbed his head Cam tripped in place Cam stamped and stomped the polished stage. Cam's face damp and blue in the spotlight. Cam's eyes lamps of white.

The girl sat against the bar. He made his way toward her. Stepped over legs, pushed past chairs and tables set with jack o'lanterns, squeezed between vampires and ghouls, the air dizzy with sweat and smoke and the rot of beer, music.

Made it to another show huh? the girl shouted.

Yeah, this place is packed, he shouted back.

Haven't missed much. She sat on two stools. She slid over.

Thanks, he shouted.

When you're with the band you're entitled to a few extras. The girl wore a leather jacket and kilt and black stockings. A floppy black velvet hat, the brim turned up. Gold hoops dangled from her ears. Hers was a face he could draw easy. What she must look like without her glasses.

I'm glad I'm not the only one who didn't wear a costume, he said. You look nice.

And you're all wet, she said and laughed. She raised her beer to her lips. Her scent drifted amid the smoke and damp. Daffodils. She had smuggled Spring into Autumn using her throat, the spots behind her ears.

Get you something? the bartender said behind them.

He turned. Bartender in Little John jerkin and soot blacked face. Skeleton hung over the bar. His eyes scanned the labels on the bottles on the wall. He said, Could I have an apple brandy?

The bartender nodded great bristly beard and turned away.

What'd you order? the girl laughed. Apple brandy? Hm. Interesting.

He laughed. Yeah, well. I like to drink it when it's wet and cold out.

Bartender big beard pushed a snifter across the bar. Two-fifty said Bartender big beard. Big bear hand scooped up bills and turned away.

He raised the snifter to his mouth. Sweet tingle from his tongue up the back of his throat to the middle of his head. He licked his lips. His face slipped to and fro in the amber pool. What had his face looked like while he dreamt under the water? And after, red and furious for air?

Is it good? she said.

He shrugged and smiled and said, I don't know. This stuff's a little mediciny, but it's okay.

Another extra I get as band moll is I can taste anyone's drink I want, the girl said. She took the snifter from his hand. Her fingernails were bitten rough. She raised the snifter to her mouth. She kissed the lip and sipped.

Mm, she said. Stuff burns my nose. Sweet though.

He said, You should try what I have at home. I make that stuff with apples from this orchard near my place.

The girl handed him the snifter. Cameron and me'll have to come try some sometime, the girl said. He wanted to say Or you could just come by yourself but she whistled loud as the music tumbled to a stop. The bar bedecked in shouts and applause. He raised the snifter to his lips. Brandy rolled across the roof of his mouth. The sweetness seeped beneath his tongue. And sheaves tied in the shapes of maidens. Sickles tossed at plaited stalks. The way she had swayed among the dead corn. The way the fire-light had caressed her thighs.

You know, she said, Cameron must think pretty highly of you. I mean he wanted you to show tonight most of all. Besides me that is.

He smiled into the glass. Ah. Cam just worries I don't get out much, he said. She laughed she slipped her arm through his. Her throat, scent. That spot where the artery danced, the stars drifted. He wanted to press his mouth to that spot. He wanted to taste the skin and prove she was made of daffodils.

Beyond the walls and windows rain. The music sawed and bumped. Cam shook and spun on stage. Cam sank to his knees and hung his head Cam sang how his love was dead, baritone cracked in despair and loss, to plead and demand and need and to want. The tearful mourner in the funeral dance. The loud lament of the disconsolate lover. But Cam had been alone with her. Cam knew she was made of flowers.

Would you look at those fucking sluts up there, the girl said. I mean even though everyone knows Cameron's my boyfriend they'd all still go to bed with him. What a bunch of shit.

Girls crowded before the stage. One girl in devil horns waved a scrap of paper at Cam.

He swilled the brandy in his glass. He cleared his throat. He said, The guys really drew a crowd tonight, huh?

She rolled her eyes and shrugged. They're not an audience, they're extras, she said. Cameron's only playing for one person.

You? he said.

Ha, she said. She raised her glass to her mouth. Don't look now but the guy in the corner over there the one in the suede jacket and oh so cool shades.

He looked.

Record producer, she said.

Wow, he said. Is he going to produce Cam's album?

Guy'd be an idiot not to I mean they had a piece on Cameron in *Jukebox* last week. There was one on the band the week before that but everyone knows Cameron's the reason the whole thing's catching on. It's like without him Pluto's Dog'd be out in the fucking garage playing high school proms and frat parties and shit but instead he's got these capitalist pig types after him trying to catch the next wave. Her hand trembled as she sipped her beer. She said, Having all those sluts up there drooling over him is just part of the scene you know.

Oh yeah, he said, It's nothing more than that. Don't worry about it. Take it from somebody who's known Cam a long time.

I'm not worried, the girl said. Love can just get kind of strange and irritating sometimes.

He drank the last of his brandy. He held up the empty snifter. He slid bills across the bar he pointed at her glass. Big Beard swept up bills, away. Cam strummed fever from his guitar. Cam sang from his place in the stars. Cam shimmied and Cam laughed. And the world.

She said, So I see Michelangelo was hard at work.

Her knee against his thigh. He shifted on his stool. What's that?

She nodded at his hands. Plaster caught beneath his nails. Plaster ground into his knuckles. Jesus you got the shit all in your hair too, she said. You sleep in this stuff or what? She brushed her fingers at his hair. She combed the hair back off his forehead. He shivered how she touched him.

She said, How did you get these scars?

He smiled. Shrugged. Well. Uh. I guess I fell out of a tree just right.

She laughed and slipped her arm through his arm. Her smell caught in his throat. He a drunk herdsman stunned at the body askew on the threshing floor. Stunned by the fury of the flail dance. By the way she'd swayed under the black sky, belly and thighs brushed by whispering corn-stalks. Her mouth open and filled with stars.

The girl said, So have you ever worked with a model?

CAM SHOUTED AND THE CROWD SHOUTED BACK. CAM BOBBED his head Cam bit his lip Cam plucked on his guitar. The girl and he on their stools at the bar. She stared into her beer. He sipped his fourth or fifth brandy. If he chewed the liqueur a little, he could make it edge drop by drop down his throat. He took another sip and smacked his lips.

Cam never told me anything about a record producer, he said. That's so. I don't know. It's pretty cool. This line up's only been together a year or so, hasn't it?

She bit her thumbnail. Spat. We'll see, she said. Who knows what'll happen I mean when something comes this easy it's got to make you worry a little don't you think?

He said, I don't know. Most things come easy to Cam. And he's never worried.

Yeah well karma catches up with everyone sooner or later.

He tapped his knee to the beat. He shrugged. Is that cynicism? he said.

Hey look I'm only optimistic when something bad is going to happen she said. She laughed and slipped her arm through his she batted her lashes. Her eyes filled with burnt brown leaves afloat in pots of honey. He smiled and looked down at her kilt. At the way her stockings stretched across her knees.

So tell me do you have a girlfriend or don't you? she said.

What's that? he hollered above the music.

She said, You heard me.

He smiled and raised the snifter to his lips. No, I don't have a girlfriend, he said. I don't really have much. I don't have any time for a relationship.

What do you mean? she said and slapped his arm. The gold hoops shook in her ears. From the looks of things you got nothing but time.

No, my work takes up a lot His reflection laughed in the brandy All my time, he said. Besides, I'm too dull to hold on to anyone for long.

She laughed and fell against him. Well, there's a sizable difference between you and Cameron.

He studied her face. The way the flat parts joined the curved parts. He could find no seam where petal joined petal. What difference is that? he said.

She said, You think you're too boring and Cameron thinks he's too irresistible. She swilled the beer in her glass. Let's face it the man can get kind of full of himself I mean he's only a singer in a minor league band. He doesn't even have a recording contract yet it's not like he's a movie star or a god or anything.

He sipped apple. Antiseptic collected in the hollows under his tongue. He swallowed and said, You don't make him sound all that irresistible.

The girl stared with those burnt autumn honey pots. She said, Don't get me wrong. He's an incredibly fantastic guy funny and sunny and all that up with people shit I mean he only ever has anything good to say about anything.

What a bastard, he said.

He's my sunny day she said. He's kind and generous but I just She took a drink I guess when we started dating I absolutely had not figured on I mean I hadn't considered the fact his music comes first before all and everything you know?

Cam the swashbuckler squeezed the microphone in one hand. Cam played his other hand over the crowd. A benediction, an invitation. A plea.

She shrugged she drank her pint. Look I know he doesn't mean to she said Hell he probably doesn't even realize it and if he does he'd never admit it but this friend of mine Sara maybe you know her she says Cam usually dates your blonde bimbo types like those mutts up front.

Well.

But obvivous, obviously I'm not like any of them.

No, he said.

You're not like any of them, he said.

And I'll never be like any of them, the girl said. So I can't help but wonder what it is about me. And wondering that reminds me Cameron's the best guy around and then I worry just how long this thing's going to last between us. She shook her head. See? Optimism at work.

Cam preened and strutted before the mike stand. Cam batted the stand between his hands and grabbed the stand and swung it over his head. Cam with eyes all glowing and white.

Look, she said, I'm just trying to say I hadn't figured on him being so committed to his thing you know I mean I guess it's one of the things that attracted me to him in the first place but I'm the type that needs lots and lots of love and attention. She pouted and fell against him. You know I'm glad you showed up. You're not really so boring as you think.

He said, I'm glad I came too. The music stomped and jangled. The glasses shook on the bar. She was luminous in that light. Face framed by leather jacket and floppy velvet hat. The large gold hoops hung from her ears.

She said, This place is cool and everything but it's too bad Cam booked the show here I mean there's no room to dance.

Yeah, he said. He stared into his glass. To tell you the truth, though, uh. Well. I guess that's part of the reason I showed up tonight.

The girl's eyes were sparks behind her hornrims. She turned toward him in the firelight, her glasses flaring onetwo against the flames. She danced and invited him to the dance. With mud on her ankles, her knees, she beckoned to him. Sickles tossed at the wedding sheaf. Raincharms thrown to drown in the stream. In the dream, in the dream, was it him or Cam cut the navel string?

He licked his lips. He said, What I mean is, all night I wanted to tell you that. At the party last month, you. Well I just wanted to say I think you're an incredible dancer. And. Well. He opened his mouth but the rest of the words swirled down his throat. Burnt leaves withered to dust. Garlic and sapphires to the mud. He raised the snifter to his lips. His nose burned.

Well thanks she said. I've always loved to dance.

Well the reason I mention it is. It's the kind of thing I, I try to capture in my work. That, that sense of movement. I.

It's freedom you know, she said. It's being free to move how you want. Society makes us give up that freedom especially women I mean we're told back straight legs crossed keep your hands folded to yourself. We're told to hate our bodies and what they can do. She bit her thumbnail. Dance though. Dance is freedom because it connects us to something before all the rules came along. Life is movement not society. Dance is anarchy.

The drums pounded Cam and bass and rhythm guitars jumping up and down hair flailing Cam howled the song clattered to an end. Cam fell over at the waist. Cam's arms dangled toward the stage, toward erupted applause, shouts of One more, Encore. Cam rose red faced Cam pulled the kerchief off his head and threw it in the crowd as the house lights went up. The crowd Awwed and Come onned but Cam handed his guitar to outstretched hands. Costumed groupies swarmed onto the stage. Cam waved toward where the girl and he sat at the bar, pointed toward the guy in suede and shades, gave the okay sign, the peace sign, the fuck you sign, and disappeared.

Looks like Cam's going to talk to the record guy, he said. He drained the snifter. He set the snifter on the bar.

The girl stared into her beer. She said, He never played me a song.

What's that?

He promised he'd dedicate me a song, she said. Cameron. Before the show.

He scratched his neck. Uh. Well. I guess he must've, uh. He shrugged. Werewolves and mummies jostled him filing past. Well, look, um. Look, I've got to get out of here now. Got some work to finish up on. Get a little more plaster in my hair, ha ha. But it was really nice to see you again. And talking.

He rose from the stool. She took hold of his arm. Wait a minute, she said.

The gold hoops quivered in her ears. Muted sparks in her eyes. She shook and shivered in the last stand of corn. She beckoned him away from the safety of the fire. Belly and thighs soft as daffodils. Daffodils soft and eager to pull him under the muddied water, the earth, to sleep. And not to awaken ever again.

Maybe I'll come pose for you sometime, she said.

17

CAM STOOD ON THE BANK OF THE BEAVER POND. THE SUN
beat down overhead. Other side of the pond a dead ash tree rose gray and
bare from the shoal. He sat and watched Cam from the sandy ledge by the
diving plank, Cam all still with his hands clasped to his chest like Cam
was praying.

Count's three and oh runners on first and third, Cam said. Cam spit
and wiped his mouth on his shoulder. At Cam's feet the open gym bag sat.
Souvenirs, Cam'd called them, when he'd unzipped the bag and showed
how it was full.

Why'd you steal all them baseballs? he'd asked Cam.

Man gets fired he wants a little something for his trouble, Cam had
said and winked.

Cam stood quiet in that bare patch on the bank. In his right hand Cam cupped a baseball. With his left Cam turned the ball real slow like the knob on a safe. The heads of the cattails moved some like they wanted to see what Cam saw across the pond.

Say man, Cam said with his hands up front of his face. Hear about the church got burned down last night?

Past Cam the bluff face broke open its mouth to dribble creek water into the pond. A monarch wings blinking floated sleepy through the canary grass. No, he said. I ain't heard nothing about it.

Huh. Guess it ain't made the rounds yet, Cam said. Winning run's up to the plate. Hitter's 3 for 4 tonight with 2 RBIs and ain't looking for the walk. The ball Cam choked with his fingers. His feet Cam scraped in the sand. But ain't it like the third or fourth church got torched now man?

From the reeds redwings chucked and sputtered. Waterlilies gave forth flowers like petaled egg innards. He said I don't know. I ain't really heard nothing.

Ain't really heard nothing, huh, Cam said. Cam rocked back on his right foot and stepped forward with his left foot turned out. Cam tucked his chin and his praying hands raised up and back of his head. Cam's right knee lifted. Cam's body shifted so Cam turned his back to him. Cam froze like this and stared across the pond.

Let me ask you, Cam said. Why do you think somebody'd go and burn a church?

The sun made him sweat to where he smelled smoke and even the tang of gasoline. How last night he hid in a tree and the fire wrapped itself all round the church and shook it side to side. How when the sirens came he jumped down from the tree and ran all the way back to Grandma's. How every time he looked over his shoulder the moon was there, watching him.

He said, I don't know why somebody'd do that. Crazy, I reckon?

Crazy, Cam said. Naw. Come on. Of all the things you could do if you was crazy. Hell. Burning a church ain't even on that list. Check it out man. You'd have to be pretty fucking pissed off to do something like that. Piss all bottled up type pissed. Acting out in a big fucking way. Ain't that more how like it is? Cam said, all still with his elbows cocked over his head and his knee raised. Cam had all the time in the world.

He watched the muscles in Cam's back and arms punch shadows in Cam's skin. He swung his feet. He stared down at his knees. The left one had got skinned somehow, maybe when he pulled himself back out the basement window. Or maybe it happened on the run home. Maybe the moon hid itself behind a tree for just a second so he tripped and fell as he ran.

He said, God alone shall judge the secrets of men.

Cam grunted. He looked and saw Cam's left leg all splayed in the air behind him, Cam's left arm flung down his body, his right elbow tucked fast to his ribs. There was a knock other side of the pond. Flickers spat from the dead gray tree. The ball bobbed on the rippled water.

Hitter's thinking fastball fastball fastball but the count goes to three and one on a slider, Cam said. Cam bent and dug a ball out the bag. Water trickled in and out the pond. The reed mace ruckled all around. Fuck though man, Cam said. Alls I know is if I'm the dude been setting fire to them churches I'd be all kinds of freaked out. Everyone wanting to get their hands on me and shit. God. Cam smiled with his spooky blue eyes. Wouldn't you be freaked man?

I don't know he said. I don't think I'd ever.

Don't think you'd do it? Cam said. Or don't think you'd get nailed? Cam rolled the ball down his arm and snapped his elbow and the ball popped up in the air. Cam caught the ball on the back of his hand and Cam just stared at him.

He looked down at the raw patch on his knee. Have no fellowship with unfruitful works of darkness, but rather reprove them, he said. For it is a shame even to speak of those things that are done of them in secret.

Cam laughed. Cam's teeth were big and straight and white. Cam said, Shit man. It's a secret why you ain't got more friends.

The sun shined on the water. The glare burned the backs of his eyes. How yesterday coming back from the pond and Roxy got him at the junked cars. Roxy in her red print dress. How Roxy'd kissed him on the neck how she did and her breath all full of liquor. He tried to put on his shirt but Roxy only pushed him so he fell back on the hood of a junker. How the heat shivered up round him. How Roxy got down and kissed his stomach and Roxy said You got pretty scars.

He kicked his feet. His throat was dry. There was a line of pain over his eye. He rubbed his forehead some and said, So you really think I, I ought to go to the prom?

Cam chuckled. Cam flipped the ball from palm to palm and Cam's eyes pushed into his eyes. Man I thought the dust settled on that crisis, Cam said. Don't tell me you're going to try and backslide after I spent all morning on you to go.

He shrugged and said, No, I. I know I said I'd go. It's just. I feel kind of dumb and all, seeing's as I ain't got a date.

Told you to take your aunt, Cam said. Guys'd think you was a real ladies' man or something, showing up with a older chick. Hell maybe you'd even get lucky.

He frowned and looked down and his face burned. How Roxy undid his cutoffs and the sun turned real slow in his eyes. I got something new for you, Roxy'd said in her red print dress. How the metal hood burnt his back and behind. How Roxy's breath was wet on his skin and all he could do was just sputter and spit like a frying egg.

Roxy ain't interested in any prom, he said. She ain't even in our school.

Cam said, Man I'm just bullshitting you, you don't got to have a date. You just got to go. Hear what I'm saying? Cam turned his back to him and scraped his feet in the sand. Cam bowed sidewise to the ash trees, his throwing hand rested on the small of his back. The baseball turned fits in Cam's fingers. Fucking A the prom, Cam said and hanged his head and laughed. I can't even believe high school's almost done for. That shit was going to go on like fuckety fuck wasn't it? Now look at us.

Yeah, he said. Can't hardly believe I start college in, in three months.

College, Cam said. That'll be cool. I guess. Cam nodded some at the trees across the pond. Cam looked to his left and round to the right like he expected to see bases with runners and people all perched up on the bluff.

He watched Cam and rubbed the hurt over his eye. He said, I wish you hadn't got. I wish you was going to school with me.

Cam raised up and sucked his breath. His hands Cam brought together like he was to pray again. Cam turned his head slow to the cattails. And slow back to the ashes. Cam's right knee lifted fast and Cam's arm swung up out down. Cam's foot splashed the shoal. The ball shot across the pond and broke sudden and hit the dead ash near water level. Flickers scattered and cut to the willows further back. The ball popped up to float on the water.

Davis's throwing hell out a them breakers tonight, Cam said. Hitter's swinging for the cheap seats but the count goes full up on a high curve. Cam swung his arms forward and back. His head Cam bent side to side. Well man. I wish you was going to college here, Cam said. Cam fetched a ball from the gym bag. Cam hawked and spit and wiped his mouth on his shoulder. But we got to do what we got to do, am I right?

Yeah, he said.

Cam tossed the ball up behind his back. The ball went over Cam's shoulder and fell in his hand. Cam said, Ain't any cause for worry though man. You'll be back. Holidays and shit. Summer vacations.

Yeah, he said.

And check it out. When you get out you got you that sweet cottage your folks left, Cam said and tossed the ball up behind his back.

He felt Cam's eyes try to pry open his head so he looked away. He rubbed his forehead and thought he smelled gasoline on his fingers. He said, I ain't ever planned to live there.

Fah. Come on sure you will.

No, he said and shook his head and dug his fingers in the sand. A dragonfly razored back and forth over the shoal. I'm going to sell it off soon as it's mine he said. That's what I'm going to do.

Whoa now wait a minute, Cam said. Cam shook the baseball at him. What the hell're you talking about? That place's fucking great man you can't sell it.

It ain't he said. I can.

Shit, Cam said, You ain't selling nothing if your grandma's got a say about it. Cam danced up on his toes and looked past the diving plank, to the break between the ash trees and the bluff. Man. I don't know what your problem is, Cam said. You can't even see it from here. The place's on the other side a the fucking cornfield. Ain't like you'd be still living at home or nothing.

He kicked his feet. A redwing dipped and arched across the pond. It ain't that, he said. It ain't that, it. It's just.

Cam said, It's just what? What the fuck is your problem man? Huh?

He pressed his hands to his head. It was like somebody put the sun in his head, but it was too big and hot and he couldn't stop the sun breaking itself out. He saw his head all black and full of cracks where the light burst through.

That's where they found my folks he said.

My folks' bodies, he said.

How yesterday the slope to Grandma's was all gold and speckled with wild carrot and dandelion. How Roxy's freckled shoulders burnt under his hands. How he tried not to yell, but Roxy made him and Roxy laughed clutching his hipbones like apples. I missed my period, he heard her say, her voice muffled by his skin. How he sat in his room all night and told Grandma through the door that he was sick and didn't want any supper and No, you can't come in. Heap on the wood and kindle the fire. Eat my flesh and burn me with fire, burn me unto the lowest hell. Compassed by sorrows, gat hold upon by the pains of hell. How last night when the moon came up and the crickets rubbed out their music in the dark and Roxy laughed and Sooner barked, he knew he would offer an offering made by fire.

So how'd you guess it, Cam? he said. How'd you guess it was me burnt them churches?

HE STARED THROUGH THE PEEPHOLE. THE FIRST CONE HAD begun to sag. He slowed the fire. Outside the ring ring of a bicycle bell. He turned toward the front door. Squeak of rusty brakes as tires crunched the gravel. He stuffed the bit of firebrick back in the peephole. He stepped from the kiln and kicked over the bucket of posts and saddles and spurs.

The bicycle fell against the tin wall bang. She a shadow in the door.

Hi, she said.

And Hi, he said.

She came into the studio, skin pink from the ride, from town. In her hair green threads of light. Sleeveless bargain blouse and faded cutoffs. Silver bracelets and green hornrims. Light flashed in the lenses.

Surprised to see me again?

Between his fingers he bent and straightened a piece of wire. Always, he said.

She laughed and tossed her bag on the scuffed piano bench. Good, she said. I have never been called predictable.

She took his arm in her arm. The back of his hand brushed her thigh. Her skin was hot. He moved his hand away. So anyways, she said, I was just sitting around the record store of all places and I said to myself This wage slave bullshit really sucks so I grabbed my stuff and jetted early. Figured you'd be out here. She smiled at him. Leaves stirred in her eyes. So what's my Michelangelo up to?

He said, Just, uh, just firing some models. The, the clay I've been using's been cracking on me. Just trying to figure out why. He looked over his shoulder. He smelled rusty with sweat. He held his arms to his sides. He said, With my luck it's probably not the clay, but the kiln.

She let go his arm and pushed past him. She went toward the back room where the kiln huffed. Sounds like a good time for you to worry about something else, she said. She turned.

The way her thighs swelled from her cutoffs. Skin flushed from the dance, from the rustle of limbs against damp dead corn. There was mud on her workboots. Mud on her shins. Mud spattered across her thighs. The way the world swam.

What're you looking at? she said. Hornrims face turned toward her legs. She pointed the toe of one foot and flexed the muscles in her thigh. She looked in his eyes.

Awful muddy, that old road, huh? he said and glanced down at the bit of wire he fumbled with his fingers.

I COULD NEVER HAVE KIDS, SHE SAID.

Come on, he said. Everybody wants kids. Don't they?

Oh my god you don't know me very well do you? she said. On the tall stool with muddy knees crossed. Feet bare. Body toward the right, face turned to his own face. Chin up, he said. She balanced a glass of apple brandy on her knee. In the glass an amber light bulb, sunlight through the brandy. She said, Shit man I can barely take care of myself the last thing in the world I need's kids. I could not even deal with a travesty like that. She shook her head and raised the glass to her lips. Shit, she said, Anyone who'd let me have kids should be publicly humiliated then shot many many times.

He squinted from her to the sketch pad. Quick darting scratches at the paper. A black finger smudged harsh line to shadow. She should have come earlier, when the light was better. Light was timeless, but bound to die. And flesh. And adoration. He brushed the charcoal across the paper.

He said, But what about the old biological clock?

Oh please, she said and rolled her eyes. She turned her head to stare out the window. Men all want the same thing but women don't we weren't all put here to become mothers you know. I sure as hell wasn't.

Sure, he said. You say that now, but the clock's still ticking.

She raised the glass to her mouth. She slurped the brandy, set the glass again on mud-streaked knee. She licked her lips. You're kind of an asshole you know that.

He smiled, slashed charcoal at the paper. The fact remains, he said.

She bounced her knee. The brandy sloshed in the glass. She said, Look I put my clock on snooze a long time ago same with the marriage thing I mean, who says I have to get married and have kids? It's just the same sad fairy tale they force down all our throats Jesus and you want to know what the totally worst thing is? When some new mother pushes me to hold her screaming brat as if I'm supposed to have some kind of meltdown by taking the thing in my arms. As if holding it was some magical spell to make me say hey! this little guy is what I've been missing all along. She watched him watch her, drawing. She said, I mean I don't even like kids why would I want any.

He rubbed the edge of his palm across the pad. He smiled and said, Because they add depth and. And meaning, to your life. Meaning meaning happiness. She rolled her eyes she sipped the light bulb in the glass. The curves of her knees and shoulders. The way the hollows of her collarbones and throat would catch the overcast light. And swell of her belly. And shadows between her thighs. He drew her naked.

Mister the only kids I want are the ones I've already got, she said. She tapped the tattoo on her shoulder. Two school children with skulls for faces, lightless eyes. The children held hands, held a balloon and cotton candy. These are all the kids I need, she said.

Don't move around so much, he said. He fumbled through the pencil box for the gum eraser. He rubbed the eraser against the pad. Stared from her to the drawing. He said, But don't you want someone to carry on your name?

If I'm married and have kids I no longer have a name. I'm either Mrs. So-and-so or just Mommy. She shivered and sipped the brandy.

But don't you want someone to live on after you're gone? Someone who. Someone to talk about who you were? You know, remember you?

If you mean do I want to be immortal well you of all people should realize I'll never die. Not when I've got you to make me into things that will last forever.

She said, It's not just the artist that lives forever through his work you know it's the model too. Yeah, she laughed. It's the model that we look at after all and anyway right? I mean you don't think of the artist when you hear the name, you think of the work. A hundred years from now they aren't going to think of you when they think of you they'll think of me. So who needs kids? A husband?

He sat back. He reached for his own glass. Tongue to swim in appled brandy. Autumn in his mouth. He said, No one's going to think of me in a hundred years.

Why do you say that? she said. And bounced her knee.

He glanced toward the window. Toward the bungalow and beyond, the fen. He said, I don't have any need for posterity. And immortality is a. It's a wasted conceit. He reached for the last joint. Lit it and inhaled. She had danced in the corn. She had beckoned him from the fire.

She sipped her glass. She said Well haven't you ever shown your work?

He watched her as he passed the charcoal over the paper. Joint in his teeth. No, he said.

Why not?

Because I don't like to be looked at, he said. I don't like to be. Studied.

That's so weak, she said, You must've dreamed of making it big. I mean

I see your stuff some of it's pretty good although a gallery friend of mine Barbara she was saying how figurative art died with the 20th century. Brancuso or somebody.

Brancusi.

Whatever, she said and her leg bounced. Haven't you ever dreamed of becoming the next Big Thing?

He puffed the joint. Beyond the open door a butterfly danced in the goldenrod. The truth and the impossibility. No, he said. I don't do this for fame and fortune.

Oh yeah right, she said. She laughed. Everybody does. Just like everybody dreams of kids and a two car garage.

He smiled and rubbed at the paper. He said, You think you're pretty clever.

A lot more than you, she said. She watched as he took another hit. So you going to let me have some of that?

He exhaled and leaned from the piano bench. He reached out his hand. Her fingers on his she took the joint. She raised it to her lips. She pouted and the tip crackled Pathways into the fen. He wanted her to dance in the rain. He wanted her to shout his name. Insane.

She passed back the joint. She blew smoke and said, So what you're saying is you're doing all this for nothing.

He shook his head. I'm not doing it for nothing.

Well what are you doing it for then?

He took another hit and passed her the joint. Smoke curled from his mouth. He shrugged. Maybe for the same reason you're here, he said and glanced at the sketchpad. Modeling, that is.

She took a drag and hissed I'm here because all my other friends are boring me to tears right now. She bounced her knee. The light bulb wobbled in her glass. He glanced from her to his naked rendering of her.

What is it you want out of life then? she said. You must want more than to just spend your days living in the middle of nowhere. At the end of a really long really bumpy really muddy road.

He laughed. The only thing that could make all this better would be a wife. Kids.

Ah, she said. She looked outside and shook her head. Light bounced off her glasses. I think what you're really saying is what would make all this better would be some sex.

He stared at the sketchpad. He cleared his throat. Uh. Well.

She arched her back, she rolled her shoulders. Her thighs moved to split her cutoffs as she leaned to hand him the roach.

She said, You know I read somewhere that art came about because of sexual desire.

He stared cross-eyed at the crackled tip orange inhale hold it Calmness Calamity now release and say, Guess there's a certain creativity inherent to both, uh. Things.

And sexual desire seeks to bury itself in images that take the object of desire from the. The. Shit how'd the book put it? Her brow furrowed. She said, From the province of the physical and put it in the realm of the imaginary. Yeah.

He stared at the pad. He wanted her to dance. He wanted to draw her while she danced, draw her kicking the leaves. Thighs brushed muddy by cornstalks. And harvest moon. And adoration.   Walk deeper, foot soundless, into the fen.

She shook her empty glass at him. She said, Artist and model is kind of a sexual thing don't you think something kind of like what's that word? Archetypal. Something kind of art – archetypal you know. Like in film.

He shook his head.

The voyeur and the exhibitionist, she said.

He nodded. He brushed the charcoal over the pad.

She bounced her knee. She held out the glass. May I please? she said. And bracelets glittered on her wrist.

He spat the dead joint and rose from the piano bench. His head a dried gourd enrattled with a few old seeds. He could not help her thighs. The mud dried and cracked. She had wanted to, but he would not let her wash off the mud.

Here's the brandy, he said. He tipped the bottle. Her glass filled.

Here's to brandy, she said. She raised the glass and sipped. Shimmer of her lips. She danced drunk and reedstalk in the mud. Apples underfoot. Mud between the toes. And nothing astounded the stars.

She smacked her lips and said, Honestly though I think it's true art and sex are like connected just like art and insanity.

He gazed in his own glass. He said, And sex and insanity?

You bet, she said. All those things go back to the unconscious mind.

He rolled his eyes.

I mean don't you ever find yourself getting aroused by your work? she said. Leaves in her eyes. Brandy glass amber light bulb on her knee. Tell the truth. Doesn't drawing me kind of turn you on? Or like when you made that clay thing of me last time I mean you said yourself you never worked with a model. Isn't it a little exciting?

The kiln mumbled hissed and hummed. They sat very close and still. Had her voice shook just slightly? He cleared his throat. I should check on. I should take a look at how the kiln's doing. It's kind of uh. Well.

She said, Can I see what you've drawn so far?

Uh, no, not yet, he said. Don't move, okay? He rose and tripped over the piano bench. She laughed behind him. He went to the back room. His hand shook as he reached for the pyrometer. Kiln furniture dashed across the cement floor. He stared into the peephole. First temperature cone collapsed. Second cone bent. Third cone only just. Sixteen hundred and sixty four degrees. He removed the tip of the pyrometer from the peephole. So tell me something, she said behind him, How come you never asked me to pose nude?

He turned. Died. She stood before the easel. He tossed the pyrometer onto the shelf he stepped on saddles and spurs. I can explain, he said.

I am here to model aren't I? she said. She smiled she slipped her arm through his arm. I mean if you're going to take my clothes off you might as well include me don't you think?

You're absolutely right, he said. Winced. No, I mean. I'm sorry, I shouldn't've done it.

You didn't even get my nipples right, she said. She laughed and squeezed his arm against her body. Her skin was hot, tacky against his own. She said, What are you afraid of?

He shrugged. Grinned foolish. I just don't know how. I mean, I didn't want you to think I was trying to. You know. Get you naked. He nodded at her glass. Get you drunk.

She said, And don't forget stoned.

Look, he said, I'm not like that, I. I wouldn't do it. Rust of sweat beneath his arms. He pulled his arms in close. I couldn't do it to Cam, he said.

She let go his arm. She leaned against the workbench. Oh. So you're saying you wouldn't ask me to pose nude because I'm dating Cameron.

Well —

Just because I complain about how much time he spends with his band doesn't mean I'm his utmost groupie.

That's not what I —

I belong to myself, she said. I don't owe anybody anything.

Sure, he said. He looked down at his hands. I didn't mean —

So if I want to model and take my clothes off that's my own damn choice not Cameron's or anybody's even yours. Well it's partly yours but. I wouldn't be here at all if I didn't want to be you know?

He said, Look, let's just say it would make me. Uneasy. To have you pose nude. I think it's enough that I can imagine details of anatomy. If you want to know the truth, I'm mainly interested in She came forward she slipped her arms around his waist In light and shadow, he said.

Put your arms around me, she said.

What? he said. Her arms around his waist. Her body pressed to his body. His nose in her hair. Daffodils.

Put your arms around me, she said. Just hold me.

He cleared his throat. He folded his arms around her. God, he said. He giggled, apple brandy.

What's funny, she whispered. In timeless light the world swam. And adoration, the flesh. So much deeper and darker than anything love could redeem.

Just this, he said. What are we doing?

She said We're doing what we want to do.

He looked in her eyes. He saw himself asleep in the tub. Saw his face afloat in the mud. Saw her thighs dance phantoms before the corn, she beckoned him from the fire. Walk deeper, foot soundless, into the fen.

Haven't you? she asked. Haven't you wanted to?

He said, But you and Cam. This isn't —

Sh, she said, and Kiss me she said, and she tilted back her head, she closed her eyes.

HE WAS CARNIVAL. SHE. TWO CLOWNS TOTTERED THEY DRUNK picked their way down the aisle of goldenrod and timothy Butterflies toward the altar of this mock wedding. They held hands.

He head a gourd dried rattled within a few apple seeds. Her white aching under the cotton wet sky. Blue veins run silent beneath lucent skin. And bra and cutoffs. She grasped his hand she dipped and spun laughing under his arm. She led him to the mouth of the fen.

Stand staring down dusty pantlegs damp from the brush of grasses. Steam rose from the floor of the chasm. Squats of cotton grass and tway-blades gathered yellow leaves from the awkward naked poplars. And dogs barked beyond the plucked cornfield.

She tucked her hair behind her ears. She sidestepped stringless manikin down the mucked embankment. White flesh trembled from split-seamed cutoffs. Her face turned toward her feet tendons riffled under the skin. Here? he wanted to ask. But here he wanted it to be. And she.

Come on, she said. She stared up at him from the slick green floor. Belly and bra and rise of steam. It's warm down here, she said.

He prodded cracked high top against the bank. Slipped grooves scratched dreams hinted brown in the mud. His foot slid from under him. He made to step down his other foot his legs spraddled Dammit knees bumpkins together thumped against the sly embankment hands squelched bats in the muck he slid on all fours down and further down into her laughter her hands.

He stared at her feet. You're right, he said. It is warm.

Her laughter rose. The sky white. He grabbed for balance at the backs of her thighs. Saw the mud smeared wet across her skin. Saw the world swim. Nothing astounded the stars.

Wait she said. Hands on his shoulders she tried to lock her knees but pulled off her feet belly soft and warm spilled over his face. He breathless mouth stuffed with daffodil trumpets and petals. His hands moved up the backs of her thighs gripped her ass the way the mud gripped the back of his head, it Envy pulled his hair. He pulled at her cutoffs.

Wait she laughed again. She belly shook in he mouth he hands pulled open she cutoffs silky panties done roped around she calves her kicked and rolled on he face her kicked off clothing rustle of weeds. Mud soaked through his workshirt. A tattoo of bones belted her waist. He tongued salt from her navel She giggled his name and pulled his hair. She pushed down his body her bra and breasts she pushed herself down until her mouth covered his mouth. Was apple brandy, was apples fallen ripe from trees, apples caught in the mud, her mouth Breath her tongue slippery on his own tongue. She sucked up the seeds that rattled in his head.

With their hands they caught up mud to spread mud laughing on each other's faces in mouth and hair she clutched his workshirt Can I? she shouted mud she tore open his shirt and buttons popped kernels of corn to the left and to the right of him. Laughtered surprise.

You've got scars she said. She traced fingers of mud over his belly.

He grabbed her wrists muddy fists clenched daffodils she tumbled in his arms so soft Oh soft and he rolled her hay bales to her back he tossed her to the mud. He struggled to his knees. Shrugged off the shirt as she on his belt smeared the buckle smeared the mud. He flipped the shirt toward a stand of comfrey and slumped the black stalks. The wet air cool across his skin and again the dogs barked. She pulled his Levis open. She pulled everything down so his own flesh pale as hers against the mud white sky.

He teetered to his feet Gots to get my shoes off and fell on his ass jolt and cold and mud and laughter. Clotted fingers toward the hightop swaddled in the folds of his levis. She reached behind her back. She unhooked her bra her breasts shook bare See you had them all wrong she laughed. Her nipples black metal in the fluorescence of the sky. Skin Venus ivory streaked with clay and yellow leaves. She slapped the mud with flat palms gathered up her hands with mud. She smeared brown circles on belly and breasts. Her ribs swelled beneath her chest. She stared with face of mud and breathed and breath and nothing astounded the stars.

He tugged at the loosened high top. He tossed it in a fern. The lace of the other was knotted double and he could not get a grip Fuck it and pulled the pantleg off his freed foot pulled the levis inside out trying to pull them off his deadbolt hightop and would not come He tried his toes to jimmy the hightop loose but no dice and no use.

She lay back Mud with her knees pulled up Hands between her thighs. Hairs curled out between her fingers. He teetered to his feet. She smiled up at him. She had somewhere lost her glasses. He stepped toward her and her knees fell Petals open to his sun. The flesh glowed blue untouched by earth a seamless dream where tendons stood out on each thigh. She smiled and cupped her hands over her pussy, her nipples black iron spangles honeyed ingots eyes, she whispered his name and he fell upon her, he pushed his hips up against her hips, fumbled for the root of his cock to put his cock inside her, but she would not move her hands, she laughed in his ear. Say please she said, and Please, he said and her hands unfolded Anthers trembled in their cups Creak of reins and rust Her took he in she fingers pressed he there His pushed into she there, just the head, just the pussy, just until he was hard enough, just then. Slowly they began, in newfound ignorance, the nature of time.

She sobbed once. Eyes squeezed shut she hooked her toes behind his calves, her arms around his shoulders, she smeared mud on his back. Her mouth bloomed like a cut. Come on, she said. He pressed his mouth to hers she mouth apple brandy. Again he kissed her, fallen apples from ripe trees, caught up apples in the mud. Fuck me, she said with her sliced apple mouth and he pushed until the end of he bumped Stars the end of she, and she sobbed again. Her bare palms slapped the mud. The children danced on her shoulder and he bit the children where they danced and strange things spun from her mouth like Have you ever eaten stars? and What was the world I had lived in? and he replied I am an artist I am a man I am a failure He was the arsonist he was the fire he was the seeker and the sought he was a fool when the tears came Yes abandoned to the mud Ah dancing round the fire Oh lost among the stars.

Her body sank in the embankment. His arms caught under her shoulders. He ground his hips against the bowl of her hips, dug her deeper in the mud. His cock burned and popped pitch the sky yawned above the black poplars, the swam world in lightless time and clay hands clutched his ass to pull him in the mud he god fucked Mud squeezed his cock and squeezed into the hollows of his mouth, leaves and apples buried to their waists in mud and monarchs clung to goldenrod and his pressed he mouth on the hole that was she mouth and Have you ever heard a flower scream?

Her was mouth a black blossum in the ground. Blossum spun and crackled stars, an old vinyl recording of horses thundered up from the dirt's spin and tilt for the one clutching daffodils in her hair Stones tumbled into the sheened blackness of horses dragging desire through the mud with corncob teeth and daffodil bulbs for eyes and squeezed her thighs around him, pulled him down and deeper down beneath vegetable and dirt, the earth with its wide ways and trees the only witnesses to testify You may kiss the bride, and it was true, beneath the mud she was his wife. Beneath the mud she was his wife. And nothing astounded the stars.

He lay on his back. Static buzzed between his thighs. The heel of his foot and the heel of his hightop dug deep in the mud. Head flung back mealy apple to the mud. He brushed cobwebs from his eyes. Blinked up-side-down up the desolate clabbered shore.

Her body dark against the white sky. A ghost fleeing its grave, seeking light. He tried to call her name, but no sound came, no voice save his breath and the barking of the dogs. He only could watch her push marshy feet up the embankment, coins kicked of mud and leaf and, as rabbits, disappear.

For the longest time. The longest time. He lay that way for the longest time. In chariot, on horseback, in entrails and in lightning he had seen the things that danced the leaves in her eyes. He had spoken to his naked self, never before seen, nor known. And he knew he knew something else he had never known, he knew he had fallen outside time, and nothing was would ever be the same.

5

GRANDMA HADN'T ATE A THING IN DAYS. CHUCK AND THE OTHERS tried but Grandma only said Let me be. She only would touch a pitcher of barley water. And the apples she buried in the mud. He asked how come Grandma wouldn't eat anything. And why'd she go and bury apples like that?

Chuck and Rob said, Grandma's just tired. She ain't sleepin too good.

He said, But how come she won't eat nothing?

That morning he got woke for Grandma was come into him and Linny's room. Grandma set candles in the windows. She took a pinch of salt from a little black sack and put it on his head. She put some on Linny's too. Grandma left. Linny brushed the salt out his hair. She's fuckin crazy Linny said. But Linny was just mad Grandma wouldn't take him to town for trick or treat.

After Grandma left he got up out the bed and ran downstairs. There was candles burned in all the windows. And a big fire in the fireplace. It was awful warm. Out front Grandma swept the porch with a broom of twigs. Grandma swept the air and her lips moved she was talking. He asked what Grandma did. And how come Grandma cried when they burnt the cornfield?

Grandma's a sad case, Roxy said.

He said, But how come she's sad?

Roxy just shrugged. Go look in her closet, Roxy said and brushed her hair.

After Chuck and everybody was gone to town for Halloween he found Grandma set down in her closet. Grandma's room all smoky and her head bent over and showed the back of her neck. She was whispering. In Grandma's closet was a little table. On it was lots of candles and a saucer of ash. There was pitchers of Ma in there too. Bunches of pitchers. Ma was pretty. Grandma didn't have any pitchers of Pa.

Grandma? he said. Grandma turned slow. She stared from inside the closet. Her eyes was wet and her face was red.

Is Ma and Pa ever comin home? he said.

Git out a here, Grandma said. Git, damn you.

HE THREW THE BALL. SOONER AND THE OTHER DOGS CHASED after. The potting shed opened creak in back of him. Grandma came out in a long black dress. Grandma had a black cloth over her head that hid her face. On her arm was a picnic basket. She had a lantern too. Grandma pulled the door to and went down the path. Grandma was singing.

Sooner and the other dogs ran up with the ball. They poked him with they noses and licked his hand. He shooed Sooner away. He went through the willows. Moss was wet under his feet. Mud got between his toes. The air was smoky for they burned the cornfield down below. It smelled sweet he liked the smell of burning corn. He liked it though it made Grandma cry.

Grandma's dress dragged on the path. The lantern swinged in her hand. Grandma was singing. He followed behind. He stopped when Grandma stopped to have up the lantern and look side to side. Grandma went past the clotheslines. Grandma went past the old well. Sooner and the other dogs whined. He lifted his hand. Hush up. Sooner and the other dogs put they belly low to the ground and wagged they tail.

He sneaked longside the brambles that marked the drop from the bluff. On tippy toe he ran under the clotheslines and jumped on his knees behind the old well. Linny always said he was going to throw him in. But there wasn't any water down there. There was only flowers grown up out in the summertime.

Grandma hanged the lantern on an apple tree. Grandma set the basket by a little table. She opened the basket. Out came a big candle Grandma lit off the lantern. Grandma took out a jar of herbs. She shook some in a saucer. She touched the candle to the saucer and a fire was there too. Grandma blew out the fire and black smoke came.

The sky was pink. It got dark. Out the basket Grandma took an apple and a pear and a potato and a corn. Each thing Grandma held up and whispered on and put on the table. Sooner and the other dogs rubbed on him behind the old well. He fell over in the crabgrass. It was wet. He pushed Sooner back.

Git damn you, he said.

Grandma got a pitcher out the basket. She whispered and poured dark stuff in a glass. Grandma took out a bunch of daffodils. White and yellow and orange. Grandma made them all year round. He liked to sit in the greenhouse till the sweet of all those flowers got him dizzy. Grandma told him stories about her daffodils. Grandma told him stories about the time she was got captured by pirates. Grandma wasn't crazy. Grandma was pretty like Ma.

The fires of the candle and the lantern got shinier. Smoke went up out the saucer. Grandma had the little black sack. She sprinkled salt round the tree. Grandma put away the sack and lifted her arms. The sleeves of her dress fell down and showed her skin. Grandma had a knife. She sang in a small voice. Sometimes her voice got big.   May these tokens of my love.   To return home this night.   Blessed be, blessed be.   Grandma danced round the apple tree the knife was shiny in her hand.

Sooner and the other dogs barked. A noise was come from the orchard.

Sooner and the other dogs barked and kicked mud running for the trees. Grandma pulled the cloth off her head. Grandma's hair all gray but before it was black.

Is it you? Grandma said to the orchard. Is it you? Sooner and the other dogs barked. Here child, Grandma said, Don't be afraid a that old hound. He hunked down behind the old well. The skin tickled on his neck. Leaves fell off the trees. A leaf went round his head it was black and poked him. It was a bat. He hollered and waved his arms and the bat squeaked. Grandma had up the lantern. There was sparks in Grandma's eyes. The knife shined in Grandma's hand.

He turned and ran.

27

MUD WAS BREAD LEAVENED BETWEEN HIS FINGERS. MUD WAS
mouths sucked wet his toes. Mud his hair. Mud his tongue. On hands and
knees he climbed out the fen.

He had wakened to bicycle tires unspooled across the gravel. To the
metal chafe of rusty brakes. And ring ring of the bell. The way he had
crouched, a shadow among the cotton grass, staring up the embankment,
without breath. The way her voice had wavered toward him across the
darkness Moonlight in a pond. Had it been real, or only a dream?

He stared back down the bank. Black currents swirled below. The goldenrod scratched his ankles. Mist brushed between his legs, beneath his
arms. The mud had warmed him in the fen, now clung Leeches to his body.
He walked toward the bungalow. Light through the kitchen window. A

dog barked across the fen.

Leaned against the veranda the bicycle. In moonlight the gleam of bell and streamers on the grips. The bits of costume jewelry glued all over, paint spattered and dripped all over, silk and plastic flowers garlanded all over the cruiser's frame.

Attached to the handlebars a basket. Basket filled with leaves. Weighted by a stone. He ruffled his hand beneath the stiff dry leaves. He pulled from the basket a man and a woman. Plastic figures off a wedding cake. The blond lick of Cam's hair. The smile on Cam's lips. The damp of Cam's lips. The wild thyme unseen and wild strawberry, laughter from the fen.

He buried husband and wife beneath the leaves. The front door stood open. He crept onto the veranda. More leaves curled on the floor. Leaves upon the bed. On the couch clothing spilled from an unzipped duffel bag. Beside the bag the leather jacket. On the floor the work boots. He picked his way among the stacks the toppled towers of books around the coffee table toward the pulse of candlelight the bathroom.

Her body sunk beneath the sudsy water. Hair slicked against her head laid back against the tub. Arms over the sides. Eyes closed. She looked tired without her glasses. And beautiful, wet. He could not swallow for his heart. Her eyes opened.

Hi, she said.

And Hi, he said.

Hope you don't mind me letting myself in, she said. She shifted and her body squeaked against the tub. I really wanted a bath and this was the best place I could think to get one.

He shook his head. He stared down into the water. Smells like cloves in here, he said.

She said, Sure it does I added clove oil to the mix. And dried flower petals honey and cinnamon extracts the usual spices. She winked. You know I take my baths very seriously.

On a stool beyond the tub a bottle and glass, appled brandy. She picked up the glass and took a drink. Mm, she said, and licked her lips. She thrust a foot up from the bubbles spilled off her ankle. So what happened to you anyway you look like you've been buried alive.

Water licked the sides of the tub. Light wickered from the candles thrust in wine bottles set on shelves on the floor around the room. Was out digging clay, he said, and glanced over his shoulder. Found this vein a while back. A good one. Stuff's like. It's almost like porcelain.

But it's been dark out for hours now, she said, And you're naked.

The candlelight wet on her shoulders. The hair slicked back on her head. He could see her in there, naked in there. He looked down at his body. At the mud concealed his flesh. A dream, was it, or something else?

He picked a grassblade from his thigh. He said Anything besides the bath bring you by?

She watched him she sipped the glass of brandy. Scooped suds in her free hand, spilled them off the edge of her palm. Petal and leaf upon her skin. Yeah actually there is something, she said. I was wondering if you've seen Cameron lately.

Cam? he said. He moved toward the sink. He would not look into the mirror. On the toilet seat her green hornrims atop her clothing. He sat back against the sink. He folded his arms.

It's so fucking strange, she said, I mean I haven't seen him in a week. I've called and left messages and stopped by his place but he's never home. Or he's not answering anyway. I talked to the other guys in the band and they say they haven't seen him but I got this feeling they're covering for him which only makes me think he's out fucking some bitch probably been in bed all week that's the kind of thing Cameron and I like to do now he's doing it with someone else.

She set the glass on the stool. She dug the heels of her hands into her eyes. Fuck I'm tired she said. You would not believe the last couple days I've had. She ran her fingers through her hair. White the suds her fingers there. Water dripped from her petaled elbows. And beyond the yellowed walls the barking of the dog.

She said, Anyhow, thought I'd hang out here with you for awhile. Leastways till the asshole turns up. I mean Cameron's not the only one who can fuck around he's not the only one who can go underground you know. She looked up at him, she looked him up and down. That's alright isn't it? I mean if I hide out here with you for a little while?

He glanced down at the linoleum. Gold the flecks in the dull pattern shifted with the candlelight shifted and tossed like sparks. Shovelheads sawblades swung. The bouchard had disappeared from his hand, the bouchard had banged the tin wall of the studio. Then glass breaking. Walk deeper, foot soundless, into the fen.

Why're you so jumpy? she said.

He shifted his ass against the sink. I'm, I'm not, I'm just, I'm, I'm kind of cold.

She said You've seen him haven't you?

The smile on Cam's mouth. The spittle on Cam's chin. Apples fallen ripe from trees, apples spilled and spinning on the mud. We must dream and we must act.

Seen him? he said.

She said, He's been by here, hasn't he?

He folded his arms. I. I don't. He leaned forward from the sink, rocked back. No, he hasn't, really. He hasn't been by here in. God. Forever.

Bastard, she said. And squeak of flesh against porcelain. The way the water licked and lapped against the tub, against her skin. And candlelight stretched the shadows.

Me? he said.

No no not you, she said and took up the glass of brandy. Fuck I bet anything he's fucking some bitch the fucking bastard hope her boyfriend catches them and beats the fuck out of him I'd love to see him crawl back to me then. She slurped from the glass.

He rocked back and forth against the sink. He stared at his cracked mud feet. Sweat trickled down his ribs. I don't know, he said. Cam's dad lives down south. Maybe could've just gone to see him.

Maybe could've just? Why wouldn't he tell someone then? Why wouldn't he tell me?

He hunched his shoulders. Cam did that kind of thing all the time, he said. Back in school. Take off to see his dad. Go camping or fishing. Not tell anyone. He shrugged and looked at the floor and rocked back and forth. He said, He'd do it, you know, so his mom'd be worried. Scared. When he came back he'd act surprised people freaked he was gone. It was. It was all a big joke to him. He shrugged and glanced at her in the dim light in the tub. She stared at him. He cleared his throat. I don't know. Maybe he figures you're someone new. Someone, someone he can play his old games on.

She stared down into the glass of appled brandy. Well either way he's an asshole she said I mean I am his lover he shouldn't treat me like I'm a skank.

You're right, he shouldn't, he. You don't deserve that.

Her hand swept back and forth the bathwater. Shovelheads and sawblades swung. The bouchard disappeared from his hand. A bottle broke across the floor.

She sighed and squinted up at him. I suppose you probably don't know his dad's number do you. You know so I can maybe call and make sure the bastard's not there.

No, he said. He folded and refolded his arms. And chafe of dried mud. I, I'm pretty sure I don't have the number. I don't even have a telephone.

Well why don't you get one then she said, sighed. She sipped the brandy. Used her finger to wipe at the rim. You would tell me if you knew where he was though wouldn't you? I mean if I was really seriously asking you?

Candlelight lolled across the floor. Mud peeled in scabs from his feet. I don't know, he said. I don't know where he is now.

She watched him with eyes dark plums. You're shivering, she said.

I, I'm cold.

Well are you just going to stand there or are you going to get in here and get cleaned up, she said. Her shoulders pale and glistened expiring suds. Her collarbones welled over with shadows.

He said, Won't I get the water all dirty?

Of course, she said, But I was muddy too, she said, From the ride down that road of yours. She spread her legs. Her knees emerged, peeled apples in the seesawed water. She hooked her elbows over the sides. Her breasts arisen nipples dark pendulums against the candlelight. Corn maiden, rye witch, wheat mother. The one not to be named. She in woman, in moon, in grain.

Get in, she said. I'll scrub your back.

He stepped into the bath. The water clasped warm around his calves. Her hands upon his waist, his shoulders. He settled between her thighs. He hunched forward he closed his eyes. In the studio, Cam faced toward the open door. Cam spoke over his shoulder, a beer in Cam's hand. Cam's voice low, confidential. What had Cam been saying?

What? he said.

Take the bucket, she said and bumped the plastic pail against his shoulder. Pour some water over your head so we can get you cleaned up. I mean it's not every day you have a gorgeous woman offering to bathe you you know.

No, he said. He pushed the bucket beneath the water. The bucket filled and he raised the bucket over his head. His arms shook as water spilled over him, his shoulders and chest. Her hands upon his head, she rubbed shampoo into his hair. Her pussy against his ass. The way her belly swelled into his back. Was it a dream, or something else?

Rinse, she said. He filled the bucket. He poured water over his head. He tasted the shampoo and cloves and mud. He rinsed again. The water turned brown, petals clung to his skin. You know you really should do something with this room she said. This whole place for that matter. It's like so absolutely depressing and claustrophobic not that I'm against those things in general but I mean for an artist you don't have much of a decorative sense do you.

Her hands scrubbed the washcloth over his back. Gooseflesh on his neck. The way the moonlight had washed the fen. And beyond the poplars the dogs had howled at him. He dropped the shovel and ran. He slipped he fell in breathless in laughter.

What do you think I should do? he said. With the place.

I don't know maybe you should paint it. Anything's better than this antacid yellow. Or why don't you put up fresh wallpaper. Add on another room. Something. Anything.

He said I guess I've thought of doing. Something. I don't know. Never really felt like I had a, a reason to. Never have any visitors. Just you. Yeah, I guess I should maybe do something. Make it more appealing to be here.

At least get rid of some of those books, she said. And pick up the tools and plaster and wood and shit I mean isn't that what you have a studio for.

You're right he said.

Of course I am she said I'm always right. Her hands on his shoulders she drew him against her chest. Soft. Oh, soft. Her hands rubbed the soapy cloth over his chest, his belly. The cloth rasped his nipples. His skin so pale, like hers. Her thighs slippery and smooth against his ribs. And breath on his neck. Scent of appled brandy. The way she bathed him, as though they were the only two. As though they were. They were. We must dream and we must act. We must take from in order to form the dreamed image. Ultimately, all art means taking a chance. But we must first learn how to gamble.

He said, Can I ask you something?

Her breath cool on his wet ear. I don't know can you.

He said, Well, I was, I've been, wondering. He stared down into the soiled water, could no longer see himself. Well, your showing up here tonight. And all we've been. Doing together. Seeing one another. Even though you're dating Cam. He coughed, cleared his throat. Laughed. I guess I've been kind of wondering if you'd ever. Do you think you'd ever leave him for me?

Lean forward, she said and she pushed him. She wrung the cloth over his back. Water dripped to water. Wax dripped and burned. His head grown dizzy as wax burned.

He closed his eyes. The bouchard swung around and around. And shovelheads and sawblades. Mud tossed in thick wet clumps, cow flop plop plopping. Apples spilled to mud. Apples sunk down deep in mud. And running breathless bloody from the fen.

He said, You'd never leave him for me, would you? But as soon as he. As soon as he turns up again, you'll go running back to him. Like I don't even matter. He shook his head. The water thick with mud. Grassblades and flower petals floated on the water. Whispers of dreams the voices of Cam laughtered from the rustled dead fireweeds.

Why do you. Why do you haunt me? he said.

Haunt you? She laughed. My god what am I a ghost?

He said If you love him so much, what is it you need from me? Why do you make me feel like. I. I feel. Why should I be your counselor when it comes to Cam?

Silence behind him. Her body crushed between his body and the tub. Softness, furious. He watched her clothing her glasses upon the toilet seat and he waited.

She reached for the glass. She sipped and passed the brandy to him. Look I don't know how to explain it, she said. She wrung the cloth out on his skin. I guess it's like Cameron's my sunny day and you, you, well you're my gray sky. I won't lie to you I love Cameron more than anyone. I don't really know how I feel about you.

He laughed. You think you love Cam. Only because you can't, you can't ever fully. Have him. Because that's just the way he is. And when he does things like this. Things that say you need him more than he needs you. Then you come and find me. Because I'm always here.

Her arms slipped under his arms to fold across his chest. She held him tight against her. He sipped sweet burn the brandy. I mean maybe some part of me needs you, she said. But see need is in a whole different place from love it's a kind of desperation you know. Need is. And it's a kind of pain.

But, love is pain, too, isn't it?

Love is sedation, she said. Love means everything's ay-okay the world is fucking alright. Need is pain. Need means you aren't getting enough enough love enough sex attention success. Whatever. Need is being unfulfilled love is fulfillment you know. It's like you know what to expect you have it all it's like And they lived happily ever after. That's love. Need is She died and He got sad and then He died. Need is tragedy. Tragedy is pain.

Need is pain, he said.

And love is sedation. Being sedated or being sedate whichever makes more sense. So when Cameron treats me like shit or sneaks off with some bitch and hides out on me, well. He fucks with my sedation. And he makes me need.

So what happens if you need and love the same person? he said.

She said, If you need and love the same person then you'll go insane.

Water dripped. Her breath moved behind him. Her belly moved with her breath. Her skin on his skin Skin infuriated him. He drank the rest of the glass. He slipped down into the bath. Soiled water caressed his chest. Candlelight moved on the ceiling. Candlewax dripped to the floor. Cam upon the floor. The smile on Cam's face. Spittle on Cam's chin. Cam had made a sound like laughter. Cam had jumped from the stool, in surprise. The beer bottle in Cam's hand burst across the floor. Cam across the floor. The way Cam's foot kicked your foot and you jumped back. The way the bouchard disappeared from your hand. Tell her what you did. Tell her before you get busted. Tell her so you won't yell it out in your sleep. Tell her so you won't have to sleep down in the fen. Tell her you did it because of her, because of her.

But he only could breathe. Dust, starch and musk. She had danced before the fire, she had pulled him beneath the mud, she his wife.

You're trembling she said.

I don't know. I don't know why, he said.

Her hand slipped down his belly, over his hip. Her fingers around his cock. He twisted in her embrace. Relax, she said. Her mouth upon his throat, she kissed him. Corn maiden, rye witch, the one not to be named. She in woman, moon and grain. He as stupefied by daffodils. Scent of daffodils the creases of her thighs. Torches lit behind his eyes. Mint the taste beneath his tongue.

Relax, she whispered, Just enjoy it. And her lips brushed back and forth his throat. And then her teeth pierced his skin. Her teeth hurt him just a little bit.

Oh, he said. And Oh, again. He was an echo, he was a reflection, he was the seed husk burst open under the dirt. Her other arm tightened across his chest while she drew and drew on his cock, while her tongue licked wet his throat So much deeper and darker than anything love could redeem and Hey she said, Are you awake? she said, Or are you asleep? she said, and Yes he said, I'm dreaming he said, I think I'm dreaming he said, and her teeth tore his skin, and Sirens wailed across the fen and Crack as the front door kicked in Here, she called out, I've got him in here, she called, We're naked in the bathtub, But he couldn't move sweet lassitude confused he limbs Appled Brandy and shovelheads sawblades swung at Fallen apples from ripe trees, sunk down apples in the mud and Why are you crying? she said, Am I hurting you? she said, and he body shook He trembled breathless bloody from the fen He slipped He fell in breathless in laughter Walk deeper Foot soundless Death a process not a moment in time and Are you going to come? she said, her mouth upon his throat She drank down the moon sparks darkness and what was it Cam had said, there, at the last? but his cock burned in her twisting grasp and he turned in her embrace, he turned and slipped, he slipped in the mud, he cried out and he slipped, he fell beneath the soiled bathwater, and he drowned.

17

COME IN, SON, COME IN, MY DON'T YOU LOOK SHARP IN THAT
tuxedo, yes, I wager you'll turn more than a few heads tonight, why, isn't it
exciting, the senior prom, a rite of passage as they say, my, you probably
thought this day would never arrive, did you, but here it is, yes, well, come in,
Son, come in, close the door behind you and take a seat, make yourself at home.

In the doorway he stood with his hands knotted before him. A fan
turned overhead. Pastor Fritz's study smelled like lemon polish. Books
covered the walls from baseboard to rafter. There were books stacked on
the floor, on the file cabinet and even on the mantle of the fireplace. The
door he pushed shut and went and sat in the leather backed chair across
from Pastor Fritz.

My, my, if that isn't a smart look, Pastor Fritz said. I used to be thin like you, ha, why, years and years ago, yes, and years upon that. Pastor Fritz wore a beige short sleeve shirt with a collar. Pastor Fritz smiled and patted his belly. Now, well, for some of us, experience can weigh on more than just the mind, ha ha, why yes.

He bowed his head and smiled. He pulled the cuffs. How Grandma'd come down from the attic with the flat plastic bag. How Grandma lay the bag on his bed and unzipped it and pulled open the flaps and there it was, Pa's tuxedo. How Grandma stood there and stared a bit at the tuxedo laid out on the bed. Going to go hang the linen to dry, Grandma had said.

Pastor Fritz blew his nose in a kerchief. Pastor Fritz's nose was red. White stubble ringed round just the back of his head. Pastor Fritz's mouth smiled under his round spectacles. So may I inquire as to your date for tonight? he said. Behind Pastor Fritz was a lead glass window. The window spilt the sunlight in colored diamonds.

He said, I. I don't. His behind he wiggled in the chair. He looked down in his lap. I don't think you know her, Pastor Fritz. I mean, her family. She ain't. She's not with the church.

Oh, Pastor Fritz said. I see. Well, I can't know everyone, now, can I? But I'm sure she's a nice young lady, at any rate, yes?

Yeah, he said. He picked at a hangnail on his thumb. The fan turned overhead. How the linens hung from the lines. How the big white sheets ached the backs of his eyes. Brambles blocked the drop off the bluff. And pollen rolled round the air. How he hollered but no answer was had from the linens.

Was there something you wanted to see me about, Sir? he said. Another book you want me to read?

Pastor Fritz said, Oh, yes, yes, of course, I'm sorry, no, no, it's not a book, not a book this time, ha ha, but rather something I'd like to discuss with you, something of a personal nature, yes, but don't worry, Son, I won't take much of your time, you have a big night ahead of you, after all.

With his finger Pastor Fritz pushed his spectacles back up his nose. Pastor Fritz smiled and cocked his head. You're a very special young man, Pastor Fritz said. In this day and age, well, it's a rarity for a youngster to be so devoted and so generous with his time. Why, just this year alone, with the food drive, the rummage sale earlier this spring, your work at the shelter. Pastor Fritz laced his thick soft fingers and leaned forward across the desk. Your kindness, well. I can only say it could not be more valuable, or appreciated.

The collar of the new shirt Grandma bought him itched his neck. His hands curled moist in his lap. I just like to help, Sir, he said and scratched at the collar. Lots of folks don't have it so good as me.

Pastor Fritz said, And yet, despite all you've done for your church and your community, work you should feel good about, I can't help but sense you're possessed of a fundamental unhappiness. The diamonds turned in the air. Pastor Fritz sat back in his chair and the chair creaked. Why, it seems there's some great burden that weighs upon you Pastor Fritz said. I find myself wondering what could possibly trouble a young man so?

The study was hot. His temples were damp with sweat. With the back of his hand he rubbed his nose and smelled the taint of gasoline. How he had crouched in Pa's tuxedo and parted the last linen like a curtain. How pollen circled round in the air. How Grandma danced round the apple tree, Grandma's hair undone.

His throat was dry and tickled some. He licked his lips. There ain't nothing wrong, he said. Serious, Sir, there ain't. There isn't. I. I just been thinking about going away to college, is all. I haven't really, I haven't ever gone away before, and. Well. He hunched down in the chair and breathed in and wondered if Pastor Fritz could smell the gasoline on him.

Pastor Fritz said, Yes, of course, the prospect of leaving home for the first time can be both exciting and, well, a little frightening, I can certainly attest to that. Pastor Fritz pushed a finger at his spectacles and smiled. But, Son, it's my feeling you've been unhappy for some time now. Are you sure college is all you have on your mind?

Yes, Sir.

Pastor Fritz frowned and sat forward in his chair. Pastor Fritz said, I hadn't wished to say anything about this, but I, well, as your pastor, and as a friend concerned for your wellbeing, I, why, I can't help but notice you haven't received Communion the last couple of services.

He stared at his hands in his lap. Diamonds glowed on the carpet near his shoe. On his shoe was a blade of grass. How Grandma'd always done things like bury apples down in the mud and put candles in all the windows and make dolls out of sheaves. The broom of twigs Grandma used to sweep the air. Even the food Grandma set out for Ma and Pa. But he'd never seen Grandma with her hair undone.

Son? Pastor Fritz said. May I ask why you haven't been receiving the sacrament?

He shrugged and stared at his hands. He said, I reckon I don't deserve it no more.

Don't deserve it? Why would you say that? said Pastor Fritz.

I just don't, he said. I don't know why I don't.

Surely, you must have your reasons, Pastor Fritz said, Something must be troubling you enough to cause you to feel this way, why, to feel undeserving of Christ's forgiveness. Has something in your bible study raised these doubts in your mind, or confused you some other way?

How Grandma rocked foot to foot with her eyes closed and held her palms flat over the ground. How she swayed round the tree and mumbled and cupped her hands like to catch rain. How Grandma made fists and shook them like rattles. Verily, verily, Grandma had said. And the linens flapped on the lines. The apple trees chattered their leaves like chimes.

No, Sir he said. I got no problem with bible study.

Well, is it possible one of my sermons disturbed you? Pastor Fritz said.

He shook his head. No, course not. It ain't nothing to do with you. It's not anything.

Sometimes the stresses of our daily life can cause old wounds to reopen, old pains to, to resurface, to remind us, if you will, Pastor Fritz said. Now, your mother and father may have passed away some time ago. But that doesn't mean it can't still hurt sometimes.

It's not anything, he said. He scratched where the collar chafed his neck.

Pastor Fritz fished around for his kerchief and blew his red nose and folded the kerchief and blew again. Pastor Fritz said, I wish you would talk to me, Son. I can't help but feel I've failed in some way to earn your trust, why, to make you comfortable enough in our relationship to confess what is bothering you. Pastor Fritz pushed at his spectacles. You understand that when we resist confessing our burdens of sin, we can live only partial lives at best, yes?

Yes, Sir.

How he wasn't sure if he'd blinked or looked away or maybe the damp linen he held over his mouth with it's smell of soap and trees had, for just a second, passed over his eyes. How pollen floated and blinked in his eyes. In her dry old hands Grandma had an ear of corn.

Flowered one, Blessed one, Grandma had said. Grandma's hair undone.

Pastor Fritz said, If it's something you've done, or if you're in trouble in some other way, why, you'll be far better off now and in the long run if you share your distress.

No he said, No, it. It ain't. I. The light came scattered through the lead glass window. Diamonds all round Pastor Fritz. There ain't nothing I can tell you, Sir.

Son, please let me help. Please tell me what's troubling you.

He stood. Gasoline vapors rose off him. Smoke puffed from the creases of Pa's tuxedo. His head was all in flames, all rushed up with flames how flames rushed up and up the churches, how the fires always rose up sudden and snatched the breath out his mouth.

My lips shall not speak wickedness, he said.

Wickedness? Son, wait, please, please, sit back down, Pastor Fritz said. I don't understand. What exactly is it that you've done?

Roxy in her red print dress. Grandma's hair undone. Roxy in her red print dress. Grandma's hair undone. How he had clutched the linen and felt all dizzy trying to figure where Grandma had got the ripened ear, though the fields weren't yet knee high. How the linen popped its pins somewhere way up in the sky.

I saw magic, he said.

Tears gummed his eyes. The doorknob poked him from behind. He reached back his hand and took hold of the knob. He saw how it would happen. Flames would roar up from the books in the walls. Smoke would roll through the vent in the floor. How Pastor Fritz's desk would creak and sway, a ball of flame. How the panes would fall out the lead glass window and the diamonds all ate up by the fire. How Grandma had just stared at him, the ear of corn in her dusty old hands. How he turned and ran.

I don't think I can come to this place no more, he said.

28

THEY WERE BURNING THE CORNFIELD BEYOND THE FEN.
The air tasted smoky, and a little sweet. He knocked loose a chunk of basalt
from the bluff. Skip of stones on the fire road below. He stared down through
the autumn leaves. He could not see it, but it was coming. The smile that
framed the kerneled teeth. The watery reptile eyes. The gun and the cuffs
and the right to remain silent.

He slipped the pitching tool the hammer into his workbelt. In moccasins he climbed the bluff. Crept along the shelf toward studio and bungalow. The crow laughed. He spun The air filled with smoke The sparks
the stars barking dogs Sirens and Time's up Come on out motherfucker.

His hands shook. Calm down, man. The pig doesn't even know you're up
here. Just sit tight and wait until he leaves. Don't make a sound.   But,

you left lights on. And doors unlocked. Shit. You'll have to beat that yellow smile back to the bungalow. Act casual. Why hello, Detective. Haven't seen you in a. What can I do for. Fuck.   Ah, but in the end all art means taking a chance. You just have to learn how to gamble.

He gripped his tools six guns hands over their mouths Remain silent he jogged parallel to the fire road. Near the bungalow he picked his way down the bluff hidden by the red yellow purple leaves. Footfalls squelched in the mud. Kicked stones. Snap of a lighter a long breath. So loud amid the autumn char the hissing cornfield. So loud. The cop could not possibly hear him cry.

He skidded down the cobbled embankment. He wiped his eyes and pushed his head through the underbrush. The cop took his time. Concerned only with stepping slow over mud around puddles. Christ you cannot hurry a stone and he slipped from the brush as the crow shouted in warning slid off the embankment to fall against the trunk of an oak. He held his breath. A thump within the bark. The thump made the purple leaves quiver. It was his heartbeat. He closed his eyes.

She had returned as the leaves died, as the fields burned, she had returned. Naked she had beckoned him toward the fen. Naked in his tub in his bed in his head. She was the daffodil that bloomed only behind his eyelids, petals unfurled to the light of his sun. Like love, sculpture is a pleasure which deepens with time, experience. As with love you must commit your entire being. You must choose a hammer which feels comfortable, not too heavy.   You must have a patient, a loving, temperament.

The way he would sit in the soapy water, waiting. Naked she'd turn her back to him she'd step into the tub. Her pale ass nestled down upon his lap. Her flesh cool at first amid the bath. His hands upon her hips, the belt of bones tattooed around her waist. Nape of her neck so luminous and soft with down. Or scabbed with mud. She moved upon him. His head fell back against the tub. Water sloshed on the floor. So warm and wet. Soft. Oh, soft. Smell of starch she skin of Daffodils and languid corn. Once or twice he had dreamed.

He peered from behind the oak. He unbuckled the tool belt he laid it at his feet. We must dream and we must act. We must not let the stone's texture color or size deter us from our goal. The crow whistled at him. He squeezed the bouchard in his hand.

The cop kicked his way closer. The cop paused to puff smoke to gaze into the cloister that was the leaves. Ceiling of shredded tapestry. A safe haven, holy place. Green in spring and summer. Resplendent in fall.

His heart thudded in the oak. He closed his eyes. Breathed the field beyond the fen. When he was a kid he.   I checked your story Son. Hate to tell you it don't wash. See we determined the girl moved in with you subsequent to Cameron's disappearance. Point of fact you two were having an affair even before he turned up missing. An affair which came to an end when Cameron and the girl got engaged. See she decided it was all over between the two of you and our guess is that this turn of events didn't set too well In fact it didn't set with you at all and since we all know everyone needs love and will take it where they can get it we concluded you were more than ready to do whatever it took to keep her but see you slipped up You should of chose a love which felt comfortable and not too heavy instead of a love that wasn't yours to keep and did I mention we compared the mud from Cameron's jeep with the samples taken from this old fire road here and you know we found similar trace elements in both samples Elements particular to this locale now Son we got suspect-motivecircumstantialevidence so why don't you just come peaceful make a full confession and the state will go easy on you First offense Unpremeditated act with an Instrument of Passion You have the right to remain silent We must dream and we must act Anything you say can and will be used against you Walk deeper foot soundless You have the right to an attorney Running breathless bloody If you cannot afford an attorney one will be appointed for you Ultimately love means taking a chance but you must first learn how to gamble Do you understand your rights as I have read them and that it is better to work directly in the stone?

He nearly cried out as the cop trudged past. Gorilla in plaid sportcoat. Ignorant on the mud. Caught up in skirting the brown puddles. In smoking his cigarette. The cop had no idea what was behind him Instrument of Passion clutched in one hand the bole of the oak in the other. Thud of silent heartbeats. Soft rattle of purple leaves. He licked his lips he breathed the sweet smoke. In moccasins he stepped away from the oak. He gripped the bouchard in his hand.

In February daffodils would grow on the shoulders of the fire road. They would line up golden trumpets heralds of the coming Spring. They would be so horrible and yellow as they laughed at him derided him like the crow and he would scream as the cop sped him downtown But isn't love like sculpture and isn't sculpture the removal of things in order to form the dreamed image and how can love allow such awful things to happen? and the cop would say Now Son, I pass no judgement, I seen how it can happen, everyone needs love, but the pain and before you know it someone ends up doing something he never thought because he's so damn and doesn't know what else to do, I seen how it can happen Son, I seen how it happened to you.

The bouchard struck the cop behind the left ear. There was a jolt in his elbow he twisted lost his footing slipped on the muddy road Splash of soiled bathwater He struggled up the hammer in his fist his breath a saw whining insane beneath the motley cloister Water trickled down his back The cop all doubled over clutching his head with one paw the other fumbling inside the plaid sport coat elbow pads the cuff grown dark with blood The moon spun tossed sparks The cop struggled inside his coat turned slow and the crow laughed and The cop turned the cop had no ear and shovelheads sawblades swung and the leaves turned to ash He'd chosen his Instrument of Passion, something comfortable yet not too heavy and as they two danced around on the mud his voice shouted down from the bluff It wasn't my fault I didn't want any of this to happen Everyone needs love yes but no one told me how and the cop turned with obsidian face and flashbulbs for eyes big hairy paw emerging from the luminous sportcoat a missionary with his cross
and Cupid carved his bow
and the cop's black crow smile of pain
burst wide an O shaped lantern of fear Oh god I am to blame I have made the world what it is Please forgive me I never wanted to hurt anyone but I didn't know what else to do and the saws and shovels whined they gnashed

their teeth Hounds impatient straining closer
and he cried
he leaped and swung
Remain silent
he raised up he swung the hammer
                                    again

5

THE TURKEY WILL BE READY SOON, GRANDMA SAID. JACK AND
Betty and the rest are on their way. Play close to the house now hear? He
ran out the back door. He leaped just like superman all the way from the
porch to the ground. He ran down the path for the woods before Grandma could holler for him to bundle up.

There was snow on the branches but the path was just muddy. He
stomped his feet in the puddles. Linny said puddles was windows to China
but he didn't believe it. He could see his face in there and he didn't live in
any China.

Past the orchard was the woodlot. There it was all tangly. He jumped
onto the tree that fell over a real long time ago. He picked the soft orange
wood. He put a piece in his mouth. He breathed deep so he could smell

the berries and moss and things that made the woodlot smell kind of rotten. Sooner barked. The other dogs too. Maybe they was fighting. He'd have to get Chuck and Rob for they was big men. They would know what to do. Chuck said he was going to take him on his first hunt this year.

He jumped down from the log and fell on his knees. He ran where Sooner and the other dogs barked. They all three tugged and snapped for a white furry thing. It was a bunny. He shouted and Sooner and the dogs dropped the bunny. He kneeled down but it didn't move. The bunny was asleep. And all red and wet. It lost one of its back legs.

Mr. Bunny Rabbit. You can stop betending now. The doggies is gone. The bunny did not move. Maybe it was cold. It sure needed a hot bath. Maybe it would like some turkey too. He picked up the bunny by the ears. They was wet and fuzzy. He would take the bunny back to Grandma's and hide it under his bed. He'd make it for his pet. He wouldn't tell anybody neither. Most of all not Linny. Linny was always keeping things for himself. Finders keeper's Linny always would say. Linny was a jerk.

He swung the bunny by the ears and Sooner and the other dogs whined at him but he just marched back to Grandma's. He said, I'll hide you in the potting shed. It's warm in there. Then when everybody's gone, I'll come get you. Okay?

There was lots of cars out front in the driveway. He wished he was a big man so he could drive a car too. When the path stopped he tiptoed behind bushes and snowmen. He jumped behind the potting shed. It was really slivery. He sometimes got slivers in his fingers. Those hurt. He peeked round the corner. Everybody went back and forth inside Grandma's. He watched them laugh and hug. That was when the mud started to eat him.

His boots went in the ground. Bunny Rabbit, look. Look what's happening he said. His pants went in the mud. His knees too. The mud was eating him. It was cold but fun.

The back door opened bang. He stopped his breath. Oh, no. He had to hide Bunny quick before anybody saw. Then he could go eat turkey. And stuffing. And a big pile of carrot raisin salad too. It was his favorite.

Chuck hollered out his name. He tried to get out the mud but it wouldn't let go. It kept pulling him down. The mud was getting colder. Chuck yelled for him to come in It's time to eat kid and then Chuck said a bad word. He pushed at the mud with his hand. That got ate too. The mud was up to the zipper on his coat. He squeezed Bunny in his other hand Bunny all red and wet and sleeping.

Boots tromped around the corner of the potting shed. He looked up. Chuck's eyes was all big and goofy and his mouth was going ahh. He laughed at Chuck's funny faces while the mud ate him. He shook Bunny and laughed. He told Chuck not to tell anyone.

BLUE SKY. AND WARM, THE SUN. TODAY DID NOT FEEL LIKE WINTER. He pulled the goggles over his eyes. He took up the circular saw in both hands. The chalk lines a blue rectangle snapped upon the back wall of the bungalow. A step ladder stood within the rectangle. He kneeled beside the ladder, before the hole drilled above the foundation. He squeezed the trigger. The blade spun.

He pushed the blade into the beveled siding. Sawdust scattered on his hands, shirt cuffs, in the air. Splinters pecked his lips, his cheeks, swarming flies. The saw vibrated through his elbows. He guided the blade up the blue line, toward the next drill hole. When he reached as high as he could, he let up on the trigger and pulled the saw from the wall. The blade scraped to a stop.

He stepped around the ladder. The orange cord slithered behind him. The sun turned in the corner of his eye, sun to sink beneath the trees. He crouched before the drill hole at the rectangle's left corner. He positioned the saw and squeezed the trigger. The blade sunk into the chalk line. Dust rained on the goggles. Dust sifted down his cuffs. He breathed the confected smell of scalded wood. He cut high as he could. She had been gone three days. The longest she'd been gone since she. And the last night he had seen her. Woke to the open door, stars. She naked stood beyond the bungalow. She stared into the fen.

What're you doing out here? he had said from the veranda, the quilt wrapped around him.

She with her arms clutched her body swaths of porcelain in the moonlight.

I heard somebody laughing down there, she said.

He said, It was just a dream. Come back to bed.

She stared down the dark. Stray branches insect limbs tangled up from the shadows of the fen. It wasn't a dream she said. I heard somebody laughing.

And the next day. And the next. And. Saw in hand he climbed the ladder. He finished the cuts he had begun on the ground. He turned the saw sidewise and raised the saw to level with his head. He held his breath. He squeezed the trigger. The blade squalled under the eaves. Dust showered him he pressed the blade into the final chalk line. The saw cut right to left, from drill hole to drill hole, and was done. He lowered the saw. He let go his breath.

He climbed down the ladder. Laid the saw on the work bench, picked up the crow bar and climbed back up. The bar wedged under the butt edge of the topmost siding. He hefted the bar he pried the board loose. Nails scritched from the studs beneath. Darkness beyond. With the bar he worked his way downward, pried loose each face. The siding he tossed to the ground. Clack clack in the warm still air.

What are you doing? she said behind him.

He turned, crow bar in hand. She flowering bride in cutoffs beside the tin outbuilding. Bicycle against her hip. His mouth damp with sweat.

He said, Was starting to wonder where you got off to.

She leaned the bicycle against the studio. I've been around, she said. She folded her arms she walked toward him. Her thighs rubbed as she walked. Light bounced in the lenses of her glasses. She paused beside the workbench. So why did you cut a hole in the wall?

He turned to the bungalow. He spat a bit of sawdust. Thought maybe I'd try to add on a room, he said. A bedroom. He kneeled and with the bar pried off the final two pieces. Hee and haw of the nails. Dust spun in the sunlight.

A bedroom? she said. Her hair cropped green in the sun. She rubbed her arms. The cast of her skin, luminous and daffodil. The way she had smeared the mud upon that skin. The way she had screamed into his mouth when she came. Walk deeper, foot soundless, into the fen.

He said, Remember a few weeks ago? You know, when you said you wished this place were bigger? He set the crowbar on the workbench. He pulled the goggles from his face. Well, I guess I kind of got it into my head to. I don't know. He tossed the goggles on the bench. I thought it might be nice to make things a little. Not so closed in. He brushed the sawdust from his hair and from his sleeves. He smiled. She said nothing.

He said Hey, I have another surprise you'll. Something you might like.

She looked off to the poplars, toward the cornfield. Her thighs blonde hairs shined in sun. What is it, she said.

Come inside, I'll show you he said. He took her hand and she let him she did not take his back. He led her around the bungalow, to the veranda green with moss. Broken pieces of wallboard stacked against the over-stuffed chair. The front door open wide. Gypsum dust trailed across the hardwood floor, from the studs, rectangled sunlight through the wall.

What is it she said. He squeezed her hand. He walked her past the sofa, past the stacks of books and sketch pads and tools, the trowel, tile cutter, rod saw, the hammer.

Take a look at this, he said. He reached his hand inside the bathroom. He flicked on the light. She leaned her head in past him.

Green the walls with trees the tendrils and vines. Grown from the baseboards white and yellow and orange daffodil. Crowns of swordfern, sprays of wild carrot, golden rod and timothy grass, reeds. Mists painted astray. Limbs dark bodies caught slipped behind runneled tree trunks. All was green. All was green and peaceful and right.

Do you like it? he said.

She pulled her hand from his. She said, I've only been gone a couple days.

Vines with berries garlanded the tub, the john, clasped the bowl of the sink. Apples peered half-hidden from the trees. She made to step inside. He caught her by the crook of her arm. The floor tiled with shucked leaves and lily pads, purple daffodil.

Finished the tiles last night he said. Have to let them set a while longer so I can caulk the joints. Seal the She pulled away from his grasp she folded her arms Seal the grout, he said. Then I. Then I just have to add the threshold.

She gazed up into the corner. Where ceiling met east and south wall, the sun. Airbrushed pale at center, golden toward the circumference. He cleared his throat. Figured after I built on the bedroom I'd paint the rest of the place the same. Have it so it would always be Spring or Summer, something, something dumb like that. He smiled and glanced at her out the corner of his eye. So, what do you think?

She turned from the bathroom, toward the hole in the wall. I don't get it she said.

He stared at the nape of her neck. He shrugged. What's there to get?

I mean why are you suddenly doing all this remodeling? Like, why now?

He glanced at the hole in the wall. Sunlight between the studs. Dust seethed in the light. He said, I, I guess I. I wanted. I want this place to be nice for you. I want you to like it here. He glanced down. Sawdust on his pantlegs.

Why? she said.

He brushed at the dust. Why? he said.

Why do you want me to like it here?

He raised his shoulders. I uh. I just thought. Since you've been kind of staying here and all, I thought maybe you'd be more comfortable if I. Fixed the place up. I don't know. He laughed.

She moved away from him, she picked her way across the room, toward the opened wall. She body diced in dusk in faded sunlight.

He said, What's wrong?

She crossed her arms. She shook her head. I'm wrong she said. I thought I was the one who didn't get it. She turned to him. He raised his shoulders again. How can you go and do things like this when you don't even know what happened? she said. I mean how can you act like things are okay when for all you know Cameron could be dead?

The wild thyme unseen and the wild strawberry, laughter from the fen. The smile on Cam's mouth. Spittle on Cam's chin. And wheelbarrow heavy with apples.

Wait a minute, he said. He moved toward her he reached out his hand. She stepped away.

She said Jesus Christ how can you possibly expect me to play house with you and be all touched by your gestures when I'm going fucking crazy?

He shook his head. I don't think we're. Playing house.

What the fuck do you call this shit? she said and flung her hand toward the hole in the wall. I guess I just didn't realize my crashing here was such a big important deal for you.

No, it's. I.

She threw her arms up she said Look I've only been hanging out here because I had this absolutely crazy idea you could help me find Cameron. I was hoping you could help me find out what happened like you might have some ideas or might know someone who'd know where to find him, something, anything, maybe? She folded her arms. Her eyes behind her glasses, damp brown leaves against a windowpane. She said, I thought out of everyone who knows him you'd be the one who'd really care.

I care, he said.

Yeah right she laughed. You haven't done shit to try and find him. You can't even be bothered to help me put up the flyers.

But, I mean, all I said was I heard those didn't work. Besides aren't the police –

Oh right yeah sure the cops, she said. I've talked way too much to those assholes and they still haven't turned up a fucking thing. Big surprise.

You've talked to them? he said. The front door stood open. When, what did you tell –

The bastards couldn't give a flying fuck about a missing musician she said. She shook her head. She turned back to the hole, the dying light. Fuck I mean I got the cops' bullshit on the one hand and, and your happy homemaking on the other. It's like nobody even wants Cameron found.

That's not true, he said behind her. I want Cam found, it's just. Look, I'm sorry I didn't realize this add on could be taken as. As bad timing. Maybe I should've said I was doing all this for myself. He took a step toward her. He folded his arms and unfolded them and scratched his neck. The truth is, I just wanted you to feel you could come here. Anytime. I wanted you to feel safe here. At least until Cam turns up. I'm sorry, I. That's the best I can –

She groaned and raked her fingers down her cheeks, her throat. Christ this whole thing is driving me absolutely insane, she said. I just want to get the hell away from here you know?

Cam's body all loose and gangly when he tried to lift Cam onto the worktable. The way Cam floundered in his grasp and he fell with Cam to the floor. The way Cam let out his breath all at once as though Cam'd been holding his breath a long time. As though Cam were only pretending.

I should probably get that hole covered up, he said. He pointed behind her. She stepped away she sat on the unmade bed. On the littered dusty floor the staple gun and roll of clear plastic. He kneeled and worried the end of the roll between his fingers. He yanked up the end. The roll unspooled across the floor. The roll bumped a stack of books. The stack toppled.

She said, Look I just came out here because I'm desperate for some peace and quiet. It's like downtown's too active there's way too much going on there's like too many people asking me about Cameron and nobody telling me a thing I don't already know.

He fished the box knife out his shirt pocket. He pushed up the blade. Turned the knife before his eyes. With his left hand he smoothed the sheet. He slid the knife across the width of the plastic. The blade made a scar in the hardwood floor. He rubbed his thumb over the scar. She sat and watched him. She said If my staying here tonight's going to be a big problem for you you should maybe just kick me out now.

He tapped the knife closed against the floor. He tossed the knife onto the dinette. He sat back on his heels. There's no problem, he said. Like I said, you can stay here whenever you want.

Good, she said. I'd hate to think about riding all the way back to town tonight. Probably get hit by a car or kidnapped or something.

He stood and shook open the sheet. He raised a corner of the plastic and stapled the corner to the top plate. He pulled taut the sheet and stapled the plastic to the plate. The bed gasped behind him. Her body close behind him. Her breath in and out. The dusty scent of daffodil. And laughter from the fen.

You know Cameron used to tell me you were in love with him, she said.

HE SWITCHED OFF THE BATHROOM LIGHT. HER BODY HUMPED up under the quilt. Her back toward him. The bed only a few feet from the hole in the wall. To his right, the coffee table piled with books and broken figurines, browned leaves spilled off the table to the floor. The bottle of apple brandy, his empty glass, her glass unfinished. The sofa under the curtained window. On the sofa her clothing.

You want the bed to yourself? he whispered.

She said, Doesn't matter. I just want sleep.

He twisted the knob on the bedside lamp. The room snapped black. The plastic sheet blue. Thumbs hooked in the waistband he slipped his underwear down his legs he stepped his feet. He lifted the quilt and slid into bed. The springs wheezed. Sheets cool and gritty with bits of dried mud, plaster. He lay on his side, close behind her. Her warmth seeped toward him. He held his breath to hear her breath. The bed creaked.

He'll be missing five weeks tomorrow, she said.

He scratched his neck. Man, he said. Doesn't even seem that long.

She swallowed. She said, Cameron's dead isn't he?

Cam smiled where Cam lay on the worktable. Cam smiled as he stretched out Cam's legs and Cam's arms. Cam smiled even when he raised the saw. And wheelbarrow heavy with apples. Barrow tipped over in the fen.

I don't know, he said, and with thumb and finger rubbed his eyes. I don't know if he's alive or dead. I don't know anything.

But do you think somebody killed him?

Moonlight through the plastic sheet. Moonlight stretched the shadows of the studs across the bed. He cleared his throat. He said, Maybe what happened was. Like an accident, or something. Spontaneous.

She rolled toward him. The bed sawed and squeaked. Her body bumped soft against his body. Smell of sweat and smell of daffodil. Her palm on his chest. Her breath hot on his throat.

But they found his jeep in that parking lot she said. I mean what kind of accident is it where they don't find any trace of you but they find your jeep all safe and sound?

His hand burned. His hand on her hip. I don't know he said. I don't know how things happen. He slid his hand over her hipbone, her ribs, to her arm. Her nakedness the softness the warmth the moon sparks darkness. He pressed his lips to her forehead. Salty to his tongue. To just put his cock inside her. All the way deep inside her. Arms and legs folded around you she pulls you under the mud. Caught to your waist in mud. To offer her the truth, like seeds borne in your hand.

Cam might still turn up, he said. You've got to. Just believe he's all right.

I've got to just find him, she said. Her breath caught on her tears. Her fingers tugged hairs on his chest. I've got to find out what happened to him because if I knew that I could at least know how to feel instead of just so fucking scared and clueless I mean not knowing anything is more awful than seeing his dead body you know?

He moved his hand to rub her back. Everything's going to be okay, he said. Her body in his arms. Hot. Damp hot under the quilt. Her breath hot wet flowers bloomed and wilted against his throat. Hot the hand that teased him with half movement, with absence, made him want to.

What? he said.

She said, Cameron was going to ask me to marry him.

The bouchard bounced off the tin wall bang. Cam got up from the stool before Cam fell to the floor. Cam and Cam's blown pupil and Cam's waxy smile. Cam upon the floor. Cam upon the worktable. Blade on the saw spun Blood down the drain spun Wheels on the barrow spun Apples dumped upon the mud. Apples all red and wet and sleeping.

How do you. How do you know he was going to ask you? he said.

She said, I just know it. A woman knows when a man is in love with her. The blood throbbed rings in his head. His breath snagged. I love you, he said. He leaned to kiss her. She turned her face away.

I really got to get some sleep, she said. She rolled over she pulled the quilt and the bed sawed beneath them. Her ass brushed his cock, her flesh cool and inconstant and maddening. He did not move. The blood swelled in his throat. Black stars swam in his eyes.

But I love you he said, and daffodils cut him with their yellow blades, petals spun and severed his limbs and his torso and his head, But I love you, he said, and daffodils filled their cups on his blood sated bulbs under the mud and Oh my god he said What I did for What I did Her breath out and in her breath slowed and died and revived with a sigh Could just she'd never wake up the way her ass just touched him and his cock burned I need   I could   I

He kicked his legs from under the quilt. He swung his feet to the floor. Skin drenched cold in the room he rose he walked to the door. Moonlight through the windows and the plastic sheet.

The latch clicked under his thumb. The sheet rustled he opened the door. Rain tapped the eaves. The welcome mat bristled under his feet. And steps of the veranda creaked. And beneath the mud she is my wife like laughter from the fen Walk deeper foot soundless to the mud the brush

of grasses

On he belly snaked down the bank of the fen. His dug he toes and squeezed the twayblades in he fists. He gouged the mud with he teeth. Rain boiled the mud. His thrust he cock down and further down God damn he said and fucked. He fucked and fucked he could not come. He fucked and fucked he foot and fist with beat the mud. He yelled he threw himself to his back. Raindrops pecked his eyes. Rain filled his mouth the way Cam's mouth dripped on the threshing floor. Bodies shadows weaved from Sheaves bodies strewn throughout the fen. Under vegetable and dirt.

In spew of sawdust and dead Offerings tossed to viscid pond water
these the Seeds clutched hidden in he hand
   The wheelbarrow heavy with apples
                            Wheelbarrow heavy
                                  with Cam
   He opened his eyes. Brass orange the sun overhung the branches of
the trees. Undulant in the rippled pondwater. Behind the water. Above
the water. He shook his head and water swirled and pressed his ears. Water
choked his lungs. He kicked his feet his ankles banged he pushed himself
from the soiled bathwater he flipped his head and coughed and coughed
with lungs full of broken glass and eyes hot marbles bugged from his
head he coughed and spit and Fuck he said.
   He fell back against the tub. He rubbed his hands over his face and he
coughed. He blew water from his nose and he coughed. He coughed and
pulled himself to his feet. Water spilled from his body to the bath. He
stepped from the tub. Water splashed the Daffodils grown from the baseboards. Daffodils scattered with the tiles on the floor.
   Drowned again, he said. He slipped on the wet he shouted he fell.
   On the floor he laughed. He said, Hey, did you hear me?
   On hands and knees he went to the next room. You here? he said.
   The bed and rumpled blankets. A pillow on the floor. No body in the
bed. No clothes on the sofa. Nothing in the closet. No sign save the plastic sheet torn from the hole in the wall. He poked his head through the
studs. No bicycle leaned against the tin outbuilding.
   He said, When are you coming back?
   He slipped between the studs. The dirt cold and gravel harsh under
his feet. The unleafed branches and the trunks of the oaks and the willows
and the poplars glistened in the sunlight. Naked and wet he hugged himself. He hunched as he walked over the gravel, around the outbuilding,
toward the mouth of the fire road. No movement down the long corridor.
Nothing high up on the bluff. Not among the firs to the left. His feet
slopped in the mud, the puddles. Mud girdled his ankles. Bicycle tracks
wavered between his feet. He shouted her name. His voice shouted back.
He turned away. He turned and turned, from bungalow to studio to fire

road, he turned and turned and wanted to ask someone what he should do, and why she had to leave, what was next.

And there, on the shoulder of the fire road, beneath the oaks, beneath the bluff, where they had always been, where they always would be no matter how many bulbs he dug up, no matter how many bulbs he chewed to paste or crushed under his heels, there, nodding gentle, staring him down, horrible daffodils.

It's Spring, he said.

17

HE DIDN'T KNOW HOW LONG CAM'D BEEN IN HIS ROOM. Sure Cam must've come through the open window, he knew that much. But it was like he'd been watching Cam watch him for a long spell before he realized it was Cam there at all. Cam with his eyes all silver reckoning in the dark. Cam's lips moist in the dark. He wished Cam'd just get it over with. Why didn't Cam just kiss him and get it over with?

You awake man? Cam said. Cam took hold of him by the shoulders. Cam shook him and his neck hurt some.

Ow, he said.

You're okay Cam said. You got a little cut is all. Just some blood.

Blood? he said. He touched his fingers to his forehead and nose and cheeks. His fingers came away black and glittered wet. There was a light on, only it was dark in the room. Only the bed was all hard and bumpy under his head. Only the light was the moon and the moon was big and full and he was lying in a road.

What happened? he said.

Come on let's set you up, Cam said. Cam got round behind him and slid his hands under his shoulders. Cam grunted Cam sat him up. His head went forward and back. He saw his feet.

I lost my shoe he said.

Cam said, You just cut your head's all. Must've been on the dome light.

I don't know man. I just know I'm in some really deep fucking shit.

He sat in the road. His legs stuck stiff out in front of him. He stared at his hand all black and wet. Blood dripped off his chin. Blood dripped black scars on his dress shirt. He had on Pa's tuxedo. He was going to the prom.

Gosh that's a awful lot of blood, he said.

There was a accident Cam said. Cam wiped his hands on his pants. Cam had lost his coat. He had lost his shoe.

Accident? he said. Poplar trees rose up all round. Him and Cam were at a bend in the road. The tail end of Cam's fastback stuck up out a drainage ditch.

Cam said, It ain't my fault I swear to God I ain't had that much to drink. There was this dog in the road all of a sudden and we just lost it. Could a happened to anybody man. It ain't my fault.

Cam stood over him Cam's shirt all blue in the moonlight. Cam's hair was mussed. Cam's eyes all wet with silver. He'd've thought Cam was an angel if it weren't for the blood on Cam's shirt.

What about the prom? he said.

Cam looked back over his shoulder. Cam looked down at him and Cam folded his arms and rocked like he was cold. She's dead, Cam said. Fuck me man. She's dead. I drug her out a the car just like I drug you.

He touched his fingers to the split in his head. Who's dead, he said.

Cam jerked his head back over his shoulder. A body was in the road. A black jacket was draped so only the legs stuck out from underneath.

Cam said, I drug her up out a there like I drug you. I tried to do something but ain't anything could be done. The car just went off the road.

Cam's girl had on both her shoes. Her legs shone white in the moon-light. She's dead? he said. He pushed himself up on his knees. He fell over on his elbows all light headed and spots swam round the dark. Cam grabbed him under the arms and pulled and blood was wet on his face and blinked in his eyes.

Shit man come on, Cam said, You're going to be okay you just cut your head is all.

How'd I lose my shoe, he said.

Cam got him on his feet. Cam pulled the kerchief out his coat pocket. Wipe your face, Cam said. He did like Cam told him but there was always more blood. It got more in his eyes. He tried to wipe careful, but blood just got in his eyes. With his finger he poked at the split sore mouth in his forehead.

Is she really dead? he said.

Him and Cam stood over the pale skinny legs stuck out on the road. The moonlight made the legs look all smooth like plaster like a department store dummy all thrust out stiff under the black jacket. Nobody could lie that still.

He patted the kerchief on his forehead. His skin was sticky under his clothes. He said, Gosh it's hot out. I'm soaked clean through. He shrugged his shoulders and Pa's coat slid down his arms. He dropped it on the road.

I got a idea, Cam said. I thought up a way out a this.

With his one hand he pressed the kerchief to his forehead. With his other hand he unfastened the bow tie and undid a couple buttons. His tee shirt was all wet. His throat was dry. The rubbing of the crickets throbbed in the still hot air.

Guess we ain't going to the prom, huh, Cam? he said.

Cam walked across the road. Cam turned and folded his arms and Cam stared down at the dummy under the jacket. Cam said, We already went.

He looked round at the poplars and up and down the road. We did? he said.

Yeah man. Then after at the motel we all drank the whisky my old man got for me. Even you had some. You actually drunk some. Cam stared at him and Cam shook his head.

The moon spun in place. From under the jacket the legs stuck out stiff like wax. We already went to the prom? he said.

Cam shook the sleeve off his wrist and Cam held out his arm. Look at my watch, Cam said. See what time it is? Prom has fucking come and gone okay? Now just listen to my idea.

He laughed and rubbed his temples. Gosh, I can't even remember. Nothing. Gosh. He looked down at his shirt. It was spotted and streaked and black with blood. He said, Grandma's going to be mad I got Pa's tuxedo all dirty.

Man shut the fuck up and let me tell you my idea, Cam said.

He stared at Cam. He tasted blood in his mouth.

Cam said, Look, I figured it out when I was pulling her up out the ditch. All we got to do is say she was driving. Check it out. You and me was too fucked up to drive. She said she was okay. She should do the driving. That was what she said. She said she was okay and she should drive. Cam raised a finger. Only she must a had too much to drink too. She said she was okay but she wasn't. She's the one drove the car off the road. Check it out. That's all we got to tell the pigs.

He said, But that ain't what happened.

Cam stamped his foot on the road. I fucking know that ain't how it happened, Cam said, It was a accident you fucking think I meant her to die?

A false witness shall not go unpunished, he said, And, and he that. He that speaketh folly, he that speaketh lies shall. Shall not escape?

Cam swore and shook his fists and spun in place beside the still white legs like Cam might trip over them. How the dummy's legs showed all funny and sad. Cam came up and grabbed him by the arms and Cam's breath was hot on his face. She's dead man and it's my fucking fault and that's got to be the worst fucking feeling anybody could ever have ever. But it was a accident. There ain't any reason I got to fuck my life up over it is there? Over a one in a million kind of fucked up mistake? She's dead and what good is it my whole life gets tossed away too?

He stared down at the funny sad legs. He said, You ain't even hurt, are you?

Cam stared with his mouth open. Cam let go his arms. Cam looked down at his own body, at the blood not Cam's blood on his shirt. Cam stared at him again. What's that got to do with anything? Cam said.

I ain't lying about what you done.

Look you ain't got to, Cam said. You can't even remember shit because you was passed out in the backseat. Check it out man all you got to say is you don't remember. I don't remember what happened officer. See? And you don't, you just said so. You ain't going to be lying man.

He said, My lips shall not speak wickedness.

Cam laughed. Cam ran his fingers through his hair and Cam laughed. So that's how it's going to fucking be huh? Cam said. Okay man. You got to do what you got to do. I can dig that. I mean you're a real stand up guy with your thou shall nots and shit. Check it out. A real honest pilgrim. Cam stepped and a rock skipped under his shoe. The moon made shadows that hid Cam's eyes. But I got to do what I got to do too, Cam said. And what I got to do is all I can to save my ass. Cut a deal with the D. A. or something. Hell. Bet I could get time off if I told the pigs who burnt them churches down. You wouldn't hold that against me now would you? Honest Abe not talking wicked and all?

He pressed the kerchief to his head. What do you mean? he said.

Cam leaned close. The silver slipped round in Cam's eyes. I'm talking a deal of our own, Cam said. I'm talking you don't know who was driving my car tonight and I don't know who burnt them churches down. Even Steven.

He said, You can't prove it was me.

I ain't got to prove shit, Cam said, That's where the pigs come in. So many folks breathing down their necks to find the firebug? Shitting well right the pigs'll prove it. Count on it man.

But Cam he said. Cam, it. I. I thought you's my friend.

I am your fucking friend, Cam said. I'm the only friend you got.

He turned away from Cam. The fastback all stove in the ditch. Past the ditch were poplars and through the poplars was a light. Roxy in her red print dress. Grandma's hair undone. He turned back to the legs stuck out from the jacket. The kerchief was wet and smelled like gasoline.

Cam said, So we got us a deal man?

Heap on wood and kindle the fire. He that is taken with accursed things shall be burnt with fire. Burneth the thickets in the wood. And burneth it at the pond. And where the priest burneth offerings upon the altar. Burneth chariots of the sun to powder. Burneth the grove, and burneth men's bones upon them, and the gates thereof where they would go. For we have made lies our refuge. Under falsehood have we hid ourselves.

We got a deal man? Cam said.

Cam didn't matter anymore, he was sure of that. What did was the legs stuck out straight on the road. The legs looked so funny. Like maybe Cam's girl slipped and fell and Cam had tossed his coat on her for laughs and time stopped just then. Or maybe the legs were props from a circus act. All he had to do was pick the legs up and juggle them. He laughed. He laughed and kicked one of the dummy's feet. He laughed again.

What the fuck're you doing? Cam said.

He kicked the foot and the foot hopped just a bit and was still. There ain't nobody under there he said. He bent and reached his hand for the jacket.

Cam threw his arms round him and pulled him away and he almost fell. Into his ear Cam said, Don't man don't. It's the worst thing you could ever want to see. Believe me she's dead she is so fucking dead. She ain't even got a face anymore.

He shook his shoulders and lunged backward into Cam's body and lunged forward and Cam let him go. He fell toward the stuck up tail of the fastback. The dirt road was packed hard under his hands and his knees and his stocking foot. He tried to remember the prom. He tried to think what the girl looked like before she found herself on the road with a coat over her. He tried to think the girl's name. What was her name? What was her name. What was.

What the fuck is so God damn funny? Cam said behind him.

This only made him laugh the more. On hands and knees he laughed until he started to cough and more spots in his eyes. He spit blood on the road and laughed. He blinked blood from his eyes and laughed. He looked over his shoulder at Cam.

I can't remember what my name is, he said.

28

RAINWATER DRIPPED FROM THE BRANCHES. THE TREE BARK
wet to his hands. In Grandma's drive a white pick up truck idled. Exhaust
huffed from the tail, hung in the air. Out of breath. His elbow ached. He
crouched behind the oak tree his hands and hightops and pantlegs blackened with mud.

The truck revved its engine. There was a metal knock and the truck
backed down the drive. Steady crunch of gravel marked by the splash of
brown puddles. The bed swung out onto the road. Clunk as gears shifted.
The truck rolled away.

He came from behind the oak. He went around to the front of the
house. In the yard stood the two maple trees. Bride and Groom. The tire
swing. Old stove and washing machine lopsided under the Bride, gutshot

and left for dead among the rusty soda cans and overgrown grasses.

He turned back to the house. Two storied blue shingle with crumbling foundation. The steps up to the weatherworn veranda. The end of a newspaper wet in the dented box Green and yellow when he was a kid. When everything had been bigger than he remembered. When the world had less secrets.

He kicked his hightops against the bottom step. He pulled the newspaper from the box. He went up the veranda he pulled open the screen door rusty brown loose hung at the top hinge. Raised his hand to knock. Reached for the latch. The hall rug stained and soiled gold. Walls painted pumpkin. Smell of damp and dust and cooked meat. The dark paneled hallway down to Grandma's room. The swayed steps to the second floor. On the right, the parlor. And to the left, the family room. Beyond, the dining room the bare banquet table, the light of the kitchen. Football game on a television.

Anybody home? he called. He pushed the door shut behind him.

Who's that? a woman's rough voice.

He stopped under the dining arch. Grandma in a wheelchair rat brown afghan draped over her shoulders. Grandma with a spoon in her hand stared at the black and white screen on the dinette before her. He stared at Grandma in the chair. Grandma with sparse white hair. Oh my Lord I can't believe it Roxy said to his left, Roxy coming from the stove, Roxy wiping hands on the apron tied across her belly.

He held up the wet newspaper. Extry, extry, he said. Grandma in a chair.

Roxy laughed and came toward him and took him in her arms. Give us some sugar Hon Roxy said and pressed her lips to his lips. Hairs poked his mouth. Her breath tasted like smoke. Body soft and fat, Roxy was not sixteen. Not since the girl in the corn. Not since the woman in his room. He did not remember this Roxy, and he fumbled out her embrace, and the house was old and small.

Roxy laughed and looked him up and down. Just look at you, Roxy said. Looks like you been partying a week straight. And skinnier'n hell. Roxy ran a hand through his damp hair. Still beautiful as ever though ain't you? Even with that pansy-ass beard, and Roxy laughed and scratched his chin and Roxy took his arm in hers. She turned toward Grandma in wheelchair and afghan. Look Ma, Roxy said. Look who's here after all these years.

Grandma looked up from the television. Gone blue eyes made Grandma look blind. Supposed to be here yesterday you Grandma said. Her chin trembled. In one hand shook the spoon of creamed peas. What the hell took so long you comin home anyhow?

I'm sorry, he said. He broke from Roxy's damp clutching hands. He kneeled beside the wheelchair. Grandma's hair so white and thin. He set the newspaper on the table and reached for the unwarm hand in her lap liverspots and gray veins You know what a, what a slow poke I can be.

Grandma watched him and gone blue eyes. If that ain't the half, Grandma said. School been out a month ain't it?

He looked up at Roxy. Roxy shrugged.

Yeah, he said. School got out last month.

Grandma said, Least you ain't been robbin me like these ones here. She thrust her hobbled chin at Roxy. I tell you how my own kin been stealin from me?

Okay Ma I told you before I heard enough a that shit, Roxy said.

Only one a my kids worth a damn was your ma. God rest her.

Roxy said, Well missy why don't you finish up your supper so we can put you to bed alright.

Grandma thrust her spoon into the green mush. I ain't a baby damn it, Grandma said. Changed all you kids diapers one right after the other.

And now I change yours, Roxy said. Roxy's hand on his shoulder. Red slippers on her feet. We had steak and red potatoes tonight, Roxy said. Those of us who wear their teeth anyhow. Want me to fix you a plate Hon?

He watched Grandma raise the shaky spoon to her mouth. He rose beside the chair. He laid his hand on Grandma's shoulder. Twigs poked through the afghan. No, he said. I couldn't eat a thing.

Roxy shook her head. Too damn skinny Hon but suit yourself. Roxy untied her apron and draped the apron on the back of a chair. Roxy pulled the afghan around Grandma's shoulders. She leaned over the table and moved the rabbit ears on the black and white. Watch the rest of the ball game okay Ma? Minnesota's winning.

S'bout time somebody won, Grandma said. Grandma pushed her spoon in the peas. S'bout time somebody won for a change.

Yeah yeah yeah Roxy said and shook her head. Roxy took his hand in her hand. She led him into the parlor. She frowned and turned his palm to the light. Your hands are filthy, Roxy laughed.

I came up the back way, he said.

Course you did Hon. I seen you creeping round out there hiding behind the trees. Waiting for Linn to leave.

He looked down at his muddied hand in her hands. Well, he said. It seemed kind of odd if I just walked up to him out of nowhere. Said hi. Wouldn't it?

Roxy said, Not any stranger than you drifting round like a ghost out there.

He sat on the davenport beside this other Roxy. In slippers and quilted housecoat. Varicose veins purple sparks on her calves. Gray wisps in her red hair. Reek of stewed flesh. Not Roxy and not him and the house squeezed smaller and smaller. His elbow throbbed.

Roxy said, Linn's been wanting to see you since he got out. Your brother misses you. He's a changed man not the asshole you grew up with. We all miss you Hon.

He picked at the mud on his hand. Roxy fished a hand in the pocket on her dress. She held up the pack Cigarette in her mouth puckered toward the lighter. She held the pack out to him.

No, he said. He glanced around the room. Potted plants in the windows. Decorative mirrors and paint by number paintings hung from the walls. Dusty knick knacks on the mantel. Over the mantel the cuckoo. Grandma's rocker. Console television and the piano no one had ever played.

He said, So. How long has, how long has Grandma been like that anyway? I mean, like. In that chair and everything. What happened to her.

Roxy puffed clouds of smoke. She said Turns out the old bird had a stroke sometime back but didn't bother telling nobody. Started wetting the bed, messing herself. Forgetting things. Like people's names. Took her in to see the doc and what do you know.

He coughed into his soiled fist. He said, Is she. Is she going to get better?

Hell no she ain't going to get better, Roxy said. God. One minute she's 72 the next she's seven. She ain't in that chair because it's all the rage. And you'd know all this if you loved her enough to come home the last ten years. Roxy raised the cigarette to her mouth. Pop of tobacco burned red in the gloom. Roxy watched him in the dim lit room.

I know it's been a long time since I've been by, he said.

Roxy laughed her horse laugh. Yeah you could say that. You could sure say that. A hell of a long time. Roxy watched him and shook her head. So just what do we owe the pleasure of your visit to anyway huh? Running for office?

I. I wanted to see how things were going. He looked toward the kitchen. I wanted to get caught up on things. You guys.

Get caught up huh. Hm. But you hid out from Linn. And missed Johnny too. Johnny. Remember him?

The cuckoo cuckooed on the wall. He stared at his muddied hands cupped in his lap. Dust around the magazines on the coffee table. I remember, he said.

Turns 11 this year, Roxy said. Good kid. Goes to school. Church. Don't get into much more trouble than blowing up frogs and tipping over cows. Quiet, keeps to himself. Probably go to college some day. Just like you. Roxy stared at him with black bulging eyes and smoked.

She said Don't worry, Johnny's staying at a friend's tonight. Just me and you Hon.

Roar from the kitchen television. And Grandma, he said.

Roxy took a drag, blew smoke. Roxy watched him. Roxy's hand on his thigh. His hands in his lap. He cleared his throat. Flames flickered here and there in the fireplace. Out the window, across the porch, sinking into the treeline, the sun.

So when did Linn get out of prison? he said.

Roxy said Oh a year ago or so. Linn's been here instead of the halfway house. It being booked solid for that big convention's in town ha ha.

He stared into his lap and frowned. What, uh. What's Linn doing these days?

What else Roxy said. Working swing at the cannery. Going to see his p.o. every week. Picking on John John and whoever else he takes a dislike to. Saying he'll fix the screen door tomorrow. Helping me out with Grandma. He's been real good with Grandma.

Well, Roxy said. With me too.

Roxy's face close to his face. Roxy's breath touched his skin. Eyes filled with grim and secret fancies for the push and pull of blood. When he was a kid and Roxy would whisper his name from the dark. Roxy's hands on him in the dark. Roxy's eyes were black. Her eyes were empty and still. He took a deep breath and coughed for all the smoke. He pushed Roxy's hand off his thigh. He shook his head but he kept right on spinning.

I don't want to hear anymore about that he said.

Aw. I thought you said you came here after all these years to get caught up on everything, Roxy said. I guess you didn't really mean everything. Well Hon why don't you just tell me why you're really here.

I. I told you. I just wanted to see. How you all were doing.

Roxy scratched the nail of her little finger across her lip. So you're sticking with that story huh? Well you know what I think it is. What with the way you was sneaking round out back. The way you're all jumpy in here. How you keep looking around like you are. I think you showed up here after all these years to see if you could hide out. The old last resort scam. I seen it all before.

He said, What're you talking about?

Roxy put her hand on his knee and leaned toward him. Her mouth close to his mouth. The way her lips glistened and hint of a smile at the corners. Burst blood vessels in her cheeks gave her a look of false vitality.

I'm sure you already know this, Roxy said, But the cops been by here looking for you.

The way the cop fell face down Bloody Sandbag to the fire road. The way he stood over the cop his arm crackling at the elbow. The bouchard dropped to the ground. The way his shouts had rained down from the cloister of the leaves.

When was he. When were the cops here?

Roxy held the cigarette between two fingers pressed it to her lips. So you know it was just the one, she said. In the early summer sometime. Smiled a lot that cop, didn't he? Gave me the creeps tell you the truth. Course what cop don't? Roxy laughed smoke and the way her belly shook under the housecoat and the way her hand squeezed his thigh.

Roxy said, First thing I thought when he shows me his badge was Uh oh Linny's got himself into some shit already. She watched him through the smoke the room was small and dim. Bet you can imagine my surprise when that pig asked for you.

The way he'd tried to lift the cop onto the dolly. The way something had gurgled in the cop's throat He gasped and dropped the cop Blood he ran and thought the cop was still alive. Blood on his hands he sank to his knees and Blood to the road and laughed.

He cleared his throat. The cop say what it was he wanted?

Roxy shook her head. Pigs don't tell you shit. Just says he's doing a official investigation and that he wants to talk to you. We tell him you ain't been by here in God knows how long and he wants to know where he can find you.

And so you told him, he said.

Roxy took a drag. Blew smoke, one eye closed, the other eye on him. So what're you wanted for?

I don't like creamed peas, Grandma hollered from the kitchen.

Roxy said, Eat em anyhow.

I'll eat em alright but you ain't gettin my money, Grandma said.

Jesus Christ if taking care a her ain't a call to sainthood I don't know what is. Roxy laughed smoke. Roxy's hand clung to his knee He could not move away.

So you told him where I was, he said. The cop.

Roxy blew smoke toward the ceiling and again with those dark bulging eyes on his eyes. Linn, Roxy said. I myself wasn't about to tell that pig nothing but Linny was worried his probation might get fucked up. You know harboring a fugitive. Not to say you done anything, just. Might be bad for Linn not to tell whatever he knows.

He glanced at the paint by numbers landscape hung on the far wall. The cuckoo over the mantle. The clock an hour fast. Roxy puffed her cigarette. He squirmed beneath her hot fat hand the cop squirmed out of his grasp so much Blood the cop had too much Blood everywhere and he wore his black rubber gloves and goggles to protect his eyes The way the sawblade kept jamming up and the cop just yawned at the ceiling and Blood flies and it's all you can do not to scream as the sick damp of Roxy's hand soaks all the way through to your skin.

So. What about it Roxy said. What did the cop want.

He scratched at his throat. His skin damp with sweat. The mud dried on his hands. Just wanted to ask me about a friend of mine's been missing. Wanted to know when I last saw him.

Uh huh, Roxy said. Okay Hon.

He cleared his throat. Did the cop say anything else? he said.

Well. Just that he remembered Grandma from way back when. He was the trooper who came to tell us about how they found your Ma and Pa. Now that you mention it he says That's the same place your nephew's livin at now ain't it and wasn't it off the interstate and wasn't that old fire road the only way in and the cop give me his card and says he says If your nephew turns up at all or if you hear anything give me a call, blah blah blah. He was like a traveling salesman or something. I tell you.

So the cop didn't say anything else.

Roxy watched him face freckled and black eyes. You're in trouble ain't you Hon Roxy said.

He picked at the mud on the back of his hands. No, he said.

Because I got are lawyer's number right here. Just say the word.

No, he said and the Cop's gone blue eyes milked up Mouth slung stupid Trousers soaked by piss He felt embarrassed for the man as he dragged the big dead body up the two steps into the studio The way the cop's arm swung toward him with the gun The way the arm swung Hand white pasty as the cop fell out his arms and fell on the ground dumb look on dumb bloody face.

I'm not in any trouble, he said.

Roxy ground out her cigarette in the big glass ashtray. Whatever you say Hon, she said. Just trying to help. That's what families're for. She moved her hand from his knee to reach for the pack. He pulled his knee away. Roxy put a cigarette in her mouth. Held out the pack. He stared.

Roxy shrugged. She said, You used to.

Snap of lighter and smoke blown in the air. The smoke stung his eyes. He glanced toward the kitchen could see the curve of the wheel of Grandma's chair and the bark and cheer from the television.

I think I want to talk to Grandma now, he said. Alone.

Alone? Roxy said. What? Why?

Alone, he said, and stood. Don't worry. I won't keep her out late.

Out late? Well now just a minute here it's getting dark out. Where the hell you think you're going to take her?

Not far, he said. I just want to talk to her. To her. Without you.

Roxy stood and took hold his arm. That ain't a good idea Hon, Roxy said. His elbow burned. She leaned her face up to his he felt her breath. It's too cold out for her. Why don't you stay here and visit with me some more?

Her breath on his skin. Eyes filled with dark and secret fancies. Nothing had changed, had only grown smaller. Older. And rust.

It's not too cold out there, he said. Can't you see I'm sweating.

He and Roxy stared at one another. The hammer swung and swung.

Roxy said, You ain't taking her nowhere.

He jerked his arm from her hand his elbow burned. He grabbed Roxy's arms in his hands and squeezed the fat dumb flesh.

Hey Roxy said. Eyes wide Roxy swore and tried to shake him loose. He squeezed harder he pushed her so she fell back on the davenport. Hey Roxy said. You knocked me down you son of a bitch.

He laughed. He said, I'm not exactly who you think I am.

He went into the kitchen. He took hold of the handles on the back of Grandma's wheelchair. Let's go for a walk, Grandma, he said. Probably been a while since you got some fresh air huh? Tears in his eyes. Grandma in a chair. He wheeled Grandma to the back door.

I'm calling the cops, Roxy said.

He laughed and pulled open the door and kicked the screen door. He pushed Grandma out onto the back porch. His heart beat in his throat. It was getting dark.

What the hell happened to you, Roxy shouted behind him.

THE RUBBER TIRES SQUEAKED FROM THE WET. HIS HIGHTOPS squished on the path. The apple trees gnawed their parts one against the other.

He said, Not too cold are you, Grandma? He pulled the afghan tighter over Grandma's shoulders. Just bones, she's just bones, God.

Why we comin all the way down here? Grandma said. Two fingers poked through the weave of the afghan. Wax melted and molded lumped and crooked.

I've been wanting to talk to my best gal, he said. You've got to admit it's been a long time since the two of us talked, you know? Way too long. He gripped the handles of the chair and pushed ahead. The wheels turned black and slick with bits of yellow grass and leaf. And dead apples scattered to the ground.

Talk? Grandma said. What're you wantin to talk about we got to come all the way down here?

Past the section of buckled fence, gray wood and rusty chicken wire. Down the path to the junked cars. Past the junked cars. Past the place where apple trees became willows, past the willows. Past the bluff walls leaned above the path. Past the bend. Past. Ridiculous the waste sad time stretched before and after.

Cranberry and leatherleaf, sweet gale and peat clumped round the beaver pond. The waters of childhood carpeted by moss and orchid and squats of weed. From the middle of the bog a branch a white arm in algae sleeve thrust stiff and dead. His elbow ached. He held his breath he pushed Grandma toward the bank.

Across the bog willows stretched shaggy trunks over the rotted carpet. The bluff a rough curve around the right and the left sides. From the sandbar the frayed diving plank bowed over the green mud. Summers and summers ago. The sun low slung purple beneath the willows, the swimming hole wet gold like the meat of a plum. Summers and summers he had stretched out on the shoal as sweet languid sleep As bodies splashed water As laughter echoed between bluff and willow, laughter to seesaw him lazy toward the sky. But when had plum water soured to rank stew as if those summers had never been? When had his past been done in?

Know how many kids learnt to swim in this old pond, Grandma said. He rubbed his elbow he hunkered down beside the chair. He reached his hand to stroke the wax fingers poked through the afghan. I'm not sure, he said. How many kids?

The old chin puckered in on hollow lips. He had never seen Grandma without teeth. He had never seen her so old. White hair and breath like moldy bath towels. Liverspots on her temples. He could blow and she'd scatter like ash to nothing. World not world.

Thirty kids Grandma said. I learnt thirty kids to swim in that beaver pond right there. Thirty damn kids in forty years. And me. Prisoner a my own house. Grandma jostled in her seat. The chair rattled. Grandma had gray hairs on her chin.

That's a lot, he said and squeezed her fingers. A lot of kids who know how to swim because of you.

Aw, you weren't too good though, Grandma said. You never liked the water never did.

He smiled. I just didn't like it when Linn held me under.

Grandma's muzzy chin puckered up and down. Her eyes blue unblinked across the beaver pond. Should see Rob's boys take to the water, Grandma said. I tell you. Frogs, those boys.

He squeezed the cold wax fingers. He blinked away the tears in his eyes and sniffed. No one does much swimming here anymore, do they?

Grandma stared. Her eyes so blue and gone the way deep blue eyes get gone. You're right, he said. He picked a leaf from the blanket. So how are. Are you getting your medicine and everything okay?

Grandma said, Only problem I gots my kids're robbin me blind. I tell you how Dolores stole my gold watch? Snatched it right off the bureau while I was asleep. Looks me straight in the eye and says she don't have it. I says to her I don't know which needs more work your thievin or your lyin but just hand my damn watch over. Grandma leaned to spit. Lord, everybody always lyin and stealin from me. Just waitin for me to die.

That ain't true, he said and squeezed the fingers. We're waitin for you to get better.

Hell you say, Grandma said. Grandma's chin buckled. You kids. Pickin the meat off my bones for I'm even cold. Snatchin the rug from under me. Ha. Well, you can bet Lloyd and Bob are fightin mad about all this. Damn if you kids won't sing another tune when Lloyd and Bob get here. Grandma rattled in her chair. Her breath listed in the air, gone blue eyes. That which was only living could only die.

Grandma said, So, why'm I out here catchin my death?

Fog curled across the bog. Laughter in the fen. On hands and knees on the fire road. Combing the underbrush for the cop's gun. The way he had grabbed up each stick and stone. The way he splashed his hands through the puddles. And turned his face to the trees and screamed. How long before he gave up on the gun? How long before he dared look at the cop again? And after such knowledge, what forgiveness?

Grandma, he said, I got to tell you about something. Something really serious and horrible that happened. I got to tell somebody what I. Something what I. He laughed. What I done.

Grandma's mouth twitched funny. And chinny chin all puckered up. You look just like your ma when she was your age, Grandma said. She pulled her good hand from the blanky Grandma touched his cheek. Same pretty face. Same fretting turn. Just like your ma, God rest her. Your ma's the one had the slim ankles.

He looked down at his hands. But I done something bad, he said.

Grandma tugged his hair. Judas Priest but if we ain't got to get you into Ned's soon. Mm mm. How'd this hair git so long anyhow? And all stringy like it ain't been washed in weeks, my. Grandma picked something from his hair. Goodness child, you been sleepin outdoors?

Please Grandma, you got to listen to me, he said. You're the only one I got left and there ain't no more time. His knees hurt from squatting he had to go pee real bad.

Grandma said Well then out with it. What's got you lookin all scairt like you are?

His chin twitched like Grandma's. He sniffled and wiped his sleeve cross his nose. See, things got real crazy, he said. No, not things, I mean. Me, I. I'm being ate alive. He licked tears salty from his mouth. I done some real bad stuff and I'm being ate alive.

What'd you go and do child? Grandma said. You the one set the potting shed on fire?

He could not speak. If Grandma found out it was him done it not Linny she'd. On hands and knees he crawled away. He crawled into the cattails and the peat slime all foamy on the bank. He lay down like to drink from the beaver pond.

On his belly he stared into the yucky water, at the fuzzy rocks that went down and down. Could see all the way to China. Could see hammers and muddy shovels. Bodies kicked over on the ground falling on the ground. Candy apples carved and sunk down in the mud. He could see his own face. I gots Ma's mouth and Pa's eyes. Gone green eyes stared under stringy bathwater.

Grandma clucked behind him. So you gone lied about the shed huh? You lied and let your own brother git the belt for somethin you done. That what you're tellin me?

Tears dropped from he face tears shivered he face in the mud. I made stuff the way it is, he said, and, I'm the bad guy, he said, and him laughed he hightops kicked on the ground. After all this time I end up being the fucking bad guy, his watched he mouth say. Watched he mouth go laughter with tears.

Where did I go wrong? Grandma said. Paid enough in my lifetime raising you kids, and this is the thanks I git. My favorite child lyin to me. No better'n all the rest. Damn. You think all I done was teach you to swim? That what you think? Well you feed and clothe 30 kids, I'm tired of it. I'm tired a you thinking I ain't done nothin. I done my best to call you home it just wasn't no use.

Stretched flat on the shoal he clutched the wet moss. To grab hold of this broke down person and plant them both under the mud. In loving embrace, to sleep. And return as daffodils in the spring.

I used to watch you in the orchard, he said.

Again the cluck cluck behind him. All your life in school, Grandma said. And for what. So you could learn how to lie to your kin? So you could burn down sheds? So you could live hand to mouth down at the old place? Forgettin all I taught you.

He watched his face. Was he real or a dream Am I myself the face I see If he was here or in the mud If I look away will I disappear for good? He face with upturned face offered he mouth hungry fish to he mouth. His reached he lips down to the green water. Cold and wet. And face smiled and face shivered away.

Sorry I burnt down the shed, he said and kicked his hightops against the ground. And I'm real real sorry I lied to you. Don't hate me, please Grandma. I didn't mean to do what I done.

What goes around'll come around, Grandma said, and coughed. The wheelchair rattled. Lord God Amighty. A prisoner in my own house.

Fog hid the willows. Rustle of wet grasses. His face wanted a kiss. The seeker and the sought. The arsonist and the fire. World not world. He touched the mud with his mouth. His face shivered and was gone.

Equinox

SHADOWS RILED THE DRIFTING CHAFF. SHADOWS FLAILED the grain. Shadows reeled to harvest drum, and humped and writhed on the threshing floor. Shadows peeled of leaf and husk, peeled to reveal her face. A shivered smoke. A cloth in a breeze. Her mouth a dark coin spun on end. The way her face disappeared her hands toward reached him. The way his shoulders shaked. His hair pulled. He laughed but he did not sound like laughter. His hair pulled the harder. His head came out the water.

What are you doing she said face caked and cracked with mud Are you fucking crazy or something?

He coughed he grabbed her wrist. She let go his hair. He turned his face and coughed against the tub. Hammers battered his ears. Stars swarmed in his sight. And mute black faces sweat red tears.

He sputtered and coughed and spat. He wiped his eyes with the heel of his hand. The bathwater licked his head. He said, You came back.

Good thing for you I did, she said. I mean if I hadn't you'd've drowned yourself I mean what the hell is going on here?

She sat sidewise to him on the tub. His feet hung over the end. His levis doughy with mud. He lifted his feet and lowered boots and all into the water. He hooked his elbows over the sides he pulled himself upright. Bathwater spilled from his hair. Bath was broth of soil and blades of grass and bract and bits of wood. The broth a glaze lapped his torso in the tub.

Why did you come back? he said.

How could I help it I left my bike at the party and fuck if I'm going back there tonight what with all the cops and everything, she said arms stretched to the sides, I mean and besides just look at me where the hell am I going to go all muddy like this anyway?

Her clothing plastered mud. Her body made of mud. Cracks for the mud dried on her arms and thighs. His dun hand against her mud knee.

No, he said. Why'd you come back to town? Tonight?

She watched him, shadows over her eyes. She said, Why else? I couldn't miss the equinox party. Though I wish now I would have. She looked away.

His scalp throbbed where she'd pulled his hair. He rubbed the sore patch on his head. Before you said you came back because you missed me, he said. He laughed.

She said, Of course I missed you. I thought about you a lot especially lately it being this time of year and all you know.

The water listed to and fro. His fingernails picked the mud on her knee. You never thought about me, he said. You only came back because of Cam.

Her brow cracked as to shed a dried skin. She glanced toward the open door. Does that surprise you? she said. Cameron's still missing after all. Why wouldn't I keep wondering and wanting to know what happened to him I mean I loved the man after all didn't I?

Time past and time present, what might have been and what has been. On his knees in the fen. Hands over his ears and the laughter. The light bulb overhead danced in the bath. Water leaked from his hair, down his face. Water made his beard itch. He picked at her knee.

He said, Do you know why the police raided the party tonight?

She looked into the bath. She shrugged. It's the risk you take for having a monster blow out she said. It's like either some local complained about the noise or the cops got tipped about all the drugs floating around the place and all the minors in possession.

He leaned his head back against the tub. He stared at the light bulb. He said, Or maybe they were looking for someone.

She looked down at him and she looked out the door. Who, she said.

He looked at his fingers. Mud made damp calluses on the tips. A detective is missing, he said. The one who was handling Cam's case. And no one knows where or what. Or why.

Beyond the walls the mud with blackened faces sighed. He picked her knee. She stared out the door. Yeah I think I heard about that on the news maybe she said But what does a missing cop have to do with the party getting busted?

His face beige smudges undulant in the bath. The arsonist and the fire. The seeker and the sought. And artist and model. Grass blades green and yellow and drifted in the water. How long had she watched him? Watched him drowning in the bath?

He picked at the mud. He said, Do you know what crazing is?

She moved her knee from his hand She frowned and shook her head. What is what? she said.

Like in ceramics. When you glaze an unfired piece. In the kiln the glaze can shrink too much and crack up into, like. Like webs, I guess. He ran his fingers to comb the hair off his face. He wiped his eyes. The water rose and fell against his chest. The trees and daffodils and swordferns on the walls. And sun up in the corner. He said, Sometimes crazing can be real. Beautiful. But it's best kept under control.

I don't know what you're saying, she said.

I'm saying I should never have met you.

Her thighs shifted where she sat on the tub. She looked toward the bathroom door. He gripped the sides of the tub. She said, Well that's a shitty thing to say.

I should never have met you, he said. I should've never. Got involved with you. He shook his head. He pulled up his knees. His levis dark and slick with water. I should've thought things out better. Never let myself think that I. That you. He shook his head again. Water trickled the curve of his jaw. You left, and I was relieved and I was. So hurt and so furious. But the months went by like they do, and I. Thought I was beginning to. Forget. But now you're back, and I realize I've never, I've never. I can't ever. He tried to smile but the corners of his mouth cracked. Christ, he said. I was so. I was so fucked without you, like. I couldn't do anything. I couldn't finish what I started. All I could do was. Remember. And now you're back. His face broke he looked away.

She said Look don't get the wrong idea. I haven't come back I mean I'm not staying I've got to leave tomorrow the San Juans and all you know.

He looked at her and he looked away. Seeds rattled hollow in his head. He said, I. I. Her hand on her thigh. He cleared his throat and wrapped his fingers around her wrist. His hand wet and pale on her curdled skin.

Why don't you tell me about your parents? he said.

She did not move. She stared at his hand. The light bulb wavered in the bath. My parents? she said and blinked. What do they have to do with.

He said, How come you never told me about your parents? Your family? He rubbed his thumb over her wrist. Why didn't you ever fill in the pieces of the puzzle?

She blinked in her mask of mud. She opened her mouth and she blinked. She closed her mouth.

He said, I never left the fen that day, the first time we. Remember, how you left me lying there? He smiled and shook his head. Water rippled against his chest. Remember how you danced? During the, the equinox, the party last year, when we. First met. God, you just. God. You put me in the fire and filled my head with cracks. God, the way you. You crazed me.

She pulled her arm. His hand tightened around her wrist.

Wait a minute, he said.

Look just let go of me, she said. You're starting to trip us both out.

The mud her wrist grew slippery in his hand. He squeezed the harder. He said, There's a crow out there that laughs like Cam. I've tried to, with my old .22, I've tried to. Find that fucking bird. But I never can. Because I've already, I've already. He blinked the tears in his eyes. He shook his head. I, I just hear it laugh. I can hear. I can hear Cam laugh. I.

She pushed herself to her feet. He rose with her from his place in the tub. Water spilled to water. Things dashed about in the burnt spinning leaves in her eyes. She pulled her arm and with her other hand she pulled his wrist. She said Let go of me right now I'm warning you goddamn it.

You were right, he said. You can need a person or you can love them. But if you need the one you love it can only mean you don't really have them. And you'll go insane. And if you go insane to have that person then you'll never have that person. Because you've lost yourself. He stepped one foot from the bath. And I lost myself. And you.

I'm going to scream, she said she yanked her arm up and down in his hand.

Just wait a minute he said Wait, please I just want to—

She swung her free arm at his head. He reached his hand and caught her wrist. She tried to get her feet under her to yank him off balance. He twisted his hips he jerked her arms past his face. Her knees knocked against the tub. She cried out. Her feet pitched behind her

and she fell

and he fell after her

into the bath

She twisted in his grasp her head banged his nose Stars in his eyes and Wait a minute, he said, Don't fight me, he said, Please don't fight me, he said, and shovelheads sawblades swung Her thighs twined around his waist and blackened faces sweat red tears Her hands clutched the tub to pull herself up and choked and Love is what goes wrong and makes the worst things happen We damn ourselves for love We damn ourselves for nothing Her thighs clenched his waist and pulled and pushed against him in the mud in the fen Thighs shuddered in soil and water in moon and fire light She coughed and eyes wide She threw herself up and down against him Mouth open her face plunged up and down the dim bath her throat caught in his hands he bore down on her

Just listen, he said

Just listen to me

Her hands flew at his face her fingers scraped his chest her throat was fury beneath his hands he held her under the rolling bath   When we mix plaster and water we loose a chain of events that cannot be stopped Her eyes through the mask of churning water she bucked and shook him between her thighs he pushed down and further down Love is what keeps me awake at night and makes me hear things in the dark like Laughter from the fen The right amount of moisture makes plaster feel creamy, silky Her fists beat his shoulders she clutched his chest and slapped him and Love will express itself anyway it can like Garlic and sapphires to the mud like Apples soft and bloated in the mud and When did we come to hate daffodils? and Why must sadness be the end of joy? and

Why couldn't you just love me? he said.

Her throat beneath his hands. A bubble drifted from her mouth. Though soil goes unturned. Though seeds become spoilt and grasses die in the blade. Too much water robs the plaster of strength. Her blind fingers. Distracted. Her fingers caressed his arms. Languid after pleasure. Lost. Her thighs loosed his waist and lost. Her hands fell from his shoulders. Her arms slipped into the bath. And nothing astounded the stars.

No, he said.

Oh no, he said.

Mouth wide she stared at him through the soiled water. The way the mud drifted scarves over her face. Her face a ghost in the bath. Her face was his face. His face as he struggled to awaken. His face unable to save itself, stupefied by daffodils. Unable to resist the ridiculous waste sad grain and flower.

Wake up, he said.

The breath sighed in and out his mouth. His nose ached his eyes stung. He rose up on his knees and dug his hands into her armpits. He pulled her from the water. Her head fell back. Her arms hung down in the bath. Scratches on his arms. Her throat Red welts made by his fingers. He hugged her to him. Her damp lips her teeth pressed to the pulse in his throat.

No, he said.

He took a breath and dragged her up on the lip of the tub. She sagged from his arms and he lunged forward his legs swung out beneath him he fell with her to the tiles. Wet fish thumped and spraddled on the tiles. He rolled her off him, to her back. He gazed on her body on the floor. The beaded water and bits of grass on her belly. Her wet thighs and cutoffs. And feet still brown with mud. He cupped the nape of her neck in his palm he pulled so her chin raised toward the ceiling. He pinched her nose in the fingers of his other hand. He leaned and breathed into her slack mouth.

Come on, wake up, he said.

You've got to wake up, he said.

He breathed in her mouth. He bit her cheek. And slapped her face. She only stared at the ceiling. Breathe, he said, Breathe breathe breathe breathe. He pressed his lips to hers. His breath pushed into her lungs. The way her belly swelled and fell. The way she stared at him. The way she stared at something that was not there.

Tell me who I am, he said.

You were supposed to tell me who I am, he said. He kissed her forehead. He pressed his cheek to hers. His fingers traced the bridge of her nose, the bow of her lips, shell of her ear.

Am I, am I more or less than a man? he said.

Am I something in between?

He kissed her cheek. He kissed the hushed artery in her throat.

Beneath the mud you are my wife, he said.

My wife by theft, he said. I stole you and. And I can never give you back. He rubbed his nose on her wet hair. Do you know how you undid me? The way you danced before the fire. The way you beckoned me and left me to, to scrape my heels at the bottom of the fen. You made me an animal dying to have you. Don't you. Don't you know you did these things to me?

The mist in her eyes. The leaves that no longer moved in her eyes. Her parted lips. Tongue pale between her teeth. Mud in streaks across her cheeks, her forehead. No seam showed where petal joined petal.

He said, Why couldn't you just love me?

He pressed his mouth to her mouth. Monarchs clung to goldenrod. Reedstalks reeled among the stars. He stretched his body on the wet floor beside her body. He wrapped his arms and legs around her. In tears he embraced her. In her cold damp ear he cried.

HOW THE BOY'S RUBBER BOOTS HAD SQUEAKED IN THE SNOW.
How the sky had been gray, there was no wind, but it was cold. How the
boy hugged the gun in his arms and hurried to keep pace. How the uncle
cradled the shotgun in one arm and lead the way into the orchard.

Dog Sooner and the others trotted alongside. Claws clicked on crusts
of snow, and tongues panted and wet noses bumped over the ground.

Crop's going to be all holed up, the uncle had said. That old some bitch
ain't going to pick up no scent.

I's awful cold, the boy had said.

How the orchard had grown rough. Apple trees gave way to the woodlot, to the tangles of thistle and buckbrush stuck up out the snow. The
uncle walked slow. The uncle stopped and started again, he walked slow.

The boy followed. It was quiet.

Weeds grew up round a willow stump. The uncle pointed a leather finger. Tromp through that grass, kid, the uncle said. Tromp it good. Never know what could be hid down in there.

The weeds cracked under the boy's boots. He hugged the gun and worried should he step on a rabbit, but there were none. Sooner and the other dogs sniffed at the snow and tracked to and fro, lickerish and panting.

Ain't nothin here, the boy said.

Come on then.

Again, the uncle walked slow. The way he would take only a few steps before stopping, looking, listening, then walking on. The way he kicked cedars where the branches touched the snow. Try that one, the uncle said and pointed. The uncle in iron pants with twine tied round the cuffs. And shooting glasses and big green vest. Loops up and down the left breast. In the loops the brass butts of the shells. In the right side of the vest the game pocket. No brace of cottontails, not yet, but chocolate bars.

I's hungry, Chuck, the boy said.

We ate breakfast not three hour ago. You ain't hungry yet.

The boy shifted the gun in his arms. He sniffed and his nose and cheeks hurt some from the cold. This gun's gettin real heavy, the boy said.

The uncle tipped the shooting glasses up onto the stocking cap. The uncle blew air out his nose and frowned. He set the shotgun against a tree. He pulled up the zipper of the game pocket. The big leather glove pushed around in the pocket and came out with a chocolate bar wrapped in silver foil. The uncle pulled a glove off with his teeth. His thick fingers tore open the foil and broke a piece of the bar. The boy smiled and took the chocolate in his mitten and pressed it to his mouth. The chocolate was cold and brittle and broke between his teeth.

The uncle said, That's all, hear?

How Sooner and the other dogs had barked. How Sooner and the other dogs had hopped back and leaped forward into a brushpile, snarling. God damn it, the uncle said, hand too late for the shotgun. A gray ball burst from the cover. The white puff of tail bobbed once up and down before it was gone. How Sooner and the other dogs had barked and chased after.

God damn it the uncle said. The uncle pulled down the zipper of the game pocket and pulled his glove back on with his teeth. God damn. Way that rabbit poured on the coal. Shit. Take forever for it to circle round. If it even will. The uncle pulled the shooting glasses down over his eyes. He looked mean behind them. You done with them sweets kid?

The boy pushed the chocolate in his mouth and, chewing, grabbed up his gun.

The uncle said, Seeing's as that damn dog's going to run that rabbit in the ground, we might as well check the trapline. Come on then.

The way the uncle's boots had kicked up bits of snow as he strode into the trees. Past scrub and bramble, through forms and squats of grass and down along the creekbed grown over with weeds. The boy followed, the gun in both arms. His boots sank into drifts of snow. The way the uncle would lean out over the creek to see here and there under the bank. How the barrel of the shotgun was used to part stiff weeds.

The uncle shook his head. Too damn cold, he said. Too damn cold.

The turmoil of the hounds had died. The trees gave way to a plowed field. None but a sheet of snow until the far black firs. The uncle walked the edge between field and wood, toward a pile of snowed over fence rails. Weeds thrust up out the rails. The uncle on his knees. The uncle set down the shotgun and went forward on his gloves. He pushed his face into a shadow in the rails.

The uncle said, Well lookee what we got here.

The uncle reached his arm into the shadow. There had been the clink of metal and a scraping sound. Don't fight now, the uncle had said. He sat back and held up the trap. Hung by its forepaws, a cottontail.

A doe, the uncle had said. Beauty ain't she.

The boy said nothing. The rabbit's hind legs curled up and kicked once or twice at the uncle's arm. The rabbit's eye blinked. Its gray hide puffed in and out. Flakes of snow in the air.

The uncle set down the trap and the chain rattled on the snow. One glove held down the rabbit as the uncle took a sap from his belt. He held it to the boy.

The boy said, What's that for?

Take it, the uncle had said and poked the boy with the sap.

Tap her on the back a the neck, the uncle had said. She won't feel nothin.

The boy stood beside the uncle. The sap heavy in the boy's hand. How the rabbit's hide had puffed fast in and out. How the rabbit's ears had tucked against its head. How its eyes had rolled up at him. The boy dropped to his knees and raised the sap.

She got her neck all bunched up the boy said. I can't.

Sure you can, the uncle said.

No I can't.

Go on. Do it. Don't be scared. She won't feel nothin.

How the boy just sat there till his eyes got red.

God damn it, the uncle said, Give me that, you. He jerked the sap from the boy's mitten. The uncle raised his arm and brought the sap down behind the rabbit's head. The rabbit's back leg kicked on the snow. Its eyes closed. The hide still. Forepaws caught in the trap. The uncle pried the jaws of the trap and pushed the jaws flat. He flipped the rabbit on its back. The way its head was twisted to the side, its mouth open a little like it was sleeping.

The boy chewed on his mitten. He said, Is she really dead?

The uncle pulled off his leather gloves and stuffed them up under the vest. Dead as dirt, the uncle said. He pulled up on the zipper of the game pocket. He pulled out a plastic bag and set it flat on the snow. From his belt the uncle took a pocketknife. We got to dress her while she's still warm, the uncle said. Don't want the meat to spoil.

The uncle pulled the blade from the knife. He held the rabbit in place with one hand and pressed the blade to the white underbelly. The boy began to cry.

What in hell's the matter with you? the uncle said.

The way the boy's sobs hung in the air. The way the snowflakes had swirled toward him across the field. The boy said, I could a had her for a pet.

The uncle snapped the blade closed. He sat back on his heels. Jesus Christ, the uncle said, It ain't no pet kid. It's food. Ain't no different than corn.

The boy grabbed the rabbit off the snow. The uncle reached for the loose ball of fur in the boy's arms. The boy hollered and hugged tighter. The uncle swore and grabbed the boy by the jacket and shook him.

Listen damn you, the uncle had said, Ain't no reason to act like a baby. We ain't harvestin for sport here. We're harvestin for what we can use. The uncle swept his arm toward the trees. This little woodlot ain't enough to feed a big crop. If we don't harvest then you got lots a little bunnies sufferin and starvin. That don't do no one no good. We're doing what's right here, the uncle had said and poked the boy hard on the chest. Now quit your cryin like a little girl.

How the snowflakes had puffed and purled all round. How they had stuck to the boy's wet lashes. The snow had made him blink, had made it hard for him to see. How the bark of Sooner and the other dogs had welled louder in the wood.

God damn it hand that over, the uncle said and shook the boy and looked from the boy to the woodlot. We got to get set up, the uncle said. If we lose that other rabbit, I swear I.

But the boy only cried harder. The tears cold on his skin. The rabbit hugged soft in his arms.

How come Ma and Pa had to die? the boy had said.

The way the uncle had only stared. The way he let go the boy's jacket and sat back on his heels. Mouth open and staring. In tears the boy had hugged the rabbit to his face. The trees had stretched black under the sky. And snow fall and bell of the hounds.

Titles available from Hawthorne Books

AT YOUR LOCAL BOOKSELLER OR FROM OUR WEBSITE : *hawthornebooks.com*

Saving Stanley: The Brickman Stories

BY SCOTT NADELSON

Oregon Book Award Winner 2004

Scott Nadelson's interrelated short stories are graceful, vivid narratives that bring into sudden focus the spirit and the stubborn resilience of the Brickmans, a Jewish family of four living in suburban New Jersey. The central character, Daniel Brickman, forges obstinately through his own plots and desires as he struggles to balance his sense of identity with his longing to gain acceptance from his family and peers. This fierce collection provides an unblinking examination of family life and the human instinct for attachment.

SCOTT NADELSON PLAYFULLY INTRODUCES *us to a fascinating family of characters with sharp and entertaining psychological observations in gracefully beautiful language, reminiscent of young Updike. I wish I could write such sentences. There is a lot of eros and humor here – a perfectly enjoyable book.* —JOSIP NOVAKOVICH
author of *April Fool's Day: A Novel*

So Late, So Soon

BY D'ARCY FALLON

This memoir offers an irreverent, fly-on-the-wall view of the Lighthouse Ranch, the Christian commune D'Arcy Fallon called home for three years in the mid-1970s. At eighteen years old, when life's questions overwhelmed her and reconciling her family past with her future seemed impossible, she accidentally came upon the Ranch during a hitchhike gone awry. Perched on a windswept bluff in Loleta, a dozen miles from anywhere in Northern California, this community of lost and found twentysomethings lured her in with promises of abounding love, spiritual serenity, and a hardy, pioneer existence. What she didn't count on was the fog.

I FOUND FALLON'S STORY *fascinating, as will anyone who has ever wondered about the role women play in fundamental religious sects. What would draw an otherwise independent woman to a life of menial labor and subservience? Fallon's answer is this story, both an inside look at 70s commune life and a funny, irreverent, poignant coming of age.* —JUDY BLUNT
author of *Breaking Clean*

HAWTHORNE BOOKS & LITERARY ARTS :: *Portland, Oregon*

God Clobbers Us All

BY POE BALLANTINE

Best American Short Story Award Winner 1998

Set against the dilapidated halls of a San Diego rest home in the 1970s, *God Clobbers Us All* is the shimmering, hysterical, and melancholy story of eighteen-year-old surfer-boy orderly Edgar Donahoe's struggles with friendship, death, and an ill-advised affair with the wife of a maladjusted war veteran. All of Edgar's problems become mundane, however, when he and his lesbian Blackfoot nurse's aide best friend, Pat Fillmore, become responsible for the disappearance of their fellow worker after an LSD party gone awry. *God Clobbers Us All* is guaranteed to satisfy longtime Ballantine fans as well as convert those lucky enough to be discovering his work for the first time.

A SURFER DUDE TRANSFORMS *into someone captivatingly fragile, and Ballantine's novel becomes something tender, vulnerable, even sweet without that icky, cloying literary aftertaste. This vulnerability separates Ballantine's work from his chosen peers. Calmer than Bukowski, less portentous than Kerouac, more hopeful than West, Poe Ballantine may not be sitting at the table of his mentors, but perhaps he deserves his own after all.* —SETH TAYLOR
San Diego Union-Tribune

Dastgah: Diary of a Headtrip

BY MARK MORDUE

Australian journalist Mark Mordue invites you on a journey that ranges from a Rolling Stones concert in Istanbul to talking with mullahs and junkies in Tehran, from a cricket match in Calcutta to an S&M bar in New York, and to many points in between, exploring countries most Americans never see as well as issues of world citizenship in the 21st century. Written in the tradition of literary journalism, *Dastgah* will take you to all kinds of places, across the world … and inside yourself.

I just took a trip around the world in one go, first zigzagging my way through this incredible book, and finally, almost feverishly, making sure I hadn't missed out on a chapter along the way. I'm not sure what I'd call it now: A road movie of the mind, a diary, a love story, a new version of the subterranean homesick and wanderlust blues – anyway, it's a great ride. Paul Bowles and Kerouac are in the back, and Mark Mordue has taken over the wheel of that pickup truck from Bruce Chatwin, who's dozing in the passenger seat. —WIM WENDERS
Director of *Paris, Texas; Wings of Desire;*
and *The Buena Vista Social Club*

HAWTHORNE BOOKS & LITERARY ARTS :: Portland, Oregon

The Greening of Ben Brown

BY MICHAEL STRELOW

Michael Strelow weaves the story of a town and its mysteries in his debut novel. Ben Brown becomes a citizen of East Leven, Oregon, after he recovers from an electrocution that has not left him dead but has turned him green. He befriends 22 year-old Andrew James and together they unearth a chemical spill cover-up that forces the town to confront its demons and its citizens to choose sides. Strelow's lyrical prose and his talent for storytelling come together in this poetic and important first work that looks at how a town and the natural environment are inextricably linked. *The Greening of Ben Brown* will find itself in good company on the shelves between *Winesburg, Ohio* and *To Kill a Mockingbird*; readers of both will have a new story to cherish.

MICHAEL STRELOW HAS GIVEN NORTHWEST READERS *an amazing fable for our time and place featuring Ben Brown, a utility lineman who transforms into the Green Man following an industrial accident. Eco-Hero and prophet, the Green Man heads a cast of wonderful and zany characters who fixate over sundry items from filberts to hubcaps. A timely raid on a company producing heavy metals galvanizes Strelow's mythical East Leven as much as the Boston Tea Party rallied Boston. Fascinating, humorous and wise,* The Greening of Ben Brown *deserves its place on bookshelves along with other Northwest classics.*

—CRAIG LESLEY
Author of *Storm Riders*

Core: A Romance

BY KASSTEN ALONSO

This intense and compact novel crackles with obsession, betrayal, and madness. As the narrator becomes fixated on his best friend's girlfriend, his precarious hold on sanity rapidly deteriorates into delusion and violence. This story can be read as the classic myth of Hades and Persephone (Core) rewritten for a twenty-first century audience as well as a dark tale of unrequited love and loneliness.

Alonso skillfully uses language to imitate memory and psychosis, putting the reader squarely inside the narrator's head; deliberate misuse of standard punctuation blurs the distinction between the narrator's internal and external worlds. Alienation and Faulknerian grotesquerie permeate this landscape, where desire is borne in the bloom of a daffodil and sanity lies toppled like an applecart in the mud.

JUMP THROUGH THIS GOTHIC STAINED GLASS WINDOW *and you are in for some serious investigation of darkness and all of its deadly sins. But take heart, brave traveler, the adventure will prove thrilling. For you are in the beautiful hands of Kassten Alonso.*

—TOM SPANBAUER
Author of *In the City of Shy Hunters*

www.hawthornebooks.com

Things I Like About America
BY POE BALLANTINE
Best American Short Story Award Winner 1998

These risky, personal essays are populated with odd jobs, eccentric characters, boarding houses, buses, and beer. Ballantine takes us along on his Greyhound journey through small-town America, exploring what it means to be human. Written with piercing intimacy and self-effacing humor, Ballantine's writings provide enter-tainment, social commentary, and completely compelling slices of life.

IN HIS SEARCH *for the real America, Poe Ballantine reminds me of the legendary musk deer, who wanders from valley to valley and hilltop to hilltop searching for the source of the intoxicating musk fragrance that actually comes from him. Along the way, he writes some of the best prose I've ever read.*   —SY SAFRANSKY
Editor, *The Sun*

September 11:
West Coast Writers Approach Ground Zero
EDITED BY JEFF MEYERS

The myriad repercussions and varied and often contradictory responses to the acts of terrorism perpetuated on September 11, 2001 have inspired thirty-four West Coast writers to come together in their attempts to make meaning from chaos. By virtue of history and geography, the West Coast has developed a community different from that of the East, but ultimately shared experiences bridge the distinctions in provocative and heartening ways. Jeff Meyers anthologizes the voices of American writers as history unfolds and the country braces, mourns, and rebuilds.

CONTRIBUTORS INCLUDE: *Diana Abu-Jaber, T. C. Boyle, Michael Byers, Tom Clark, Joshua Clover, Peter Coyote, John Daniel, Harlan Ellison, Lawrence Ferlinghetti, Amy Gerstler, Lawrence Grobel, Ehud Havazelet, Ken Kesey, Maxine Hong Kingston, Stacey Levine, Tom Spanbauer, Primus St. John, Sallie Tisdale, Alice Walker, and many others.*

HAWTHORNE BOOKS & LITERARY ARTS :: *Portland, Oregon*